Crystal Saga

7 - *Looking Forward...*
and Backward

8 – *Making Progress*

D. E. Weingand

Crystal Saga

7 - Looking Forward . . . and Backward
8 - Making Progress
A Crystal Saga Series

ISBN: 978-0-578-29203-8

Published by D. E. Weingand, Florence, Oregon 97439.

Printed in the United States of America.

Front cover photo by D. E. Weingand.

Luanna K. Leisure, Little White Feather
Graphic Artist and Independent Publisher.

To order additional books go to: **http://www.LuLu.com, Amazon.com or Barnesandnoble.com**

Email: weingand@me.com

Looking Forward . . . and Backward
A Crystal Saga Series
Book 7

Table of Contents

Making Progress
A Crystal Saga Series
Book 8

Table of Contents

Cast of Characters

Tamara…Heroine and Queen of Marinea

Terra…Tamara's mother

Trident…Tamara's father and a prince and King of Marinea

Trillium…Trident's twin

Trina…Tamara's sister

Mia…Tamara's personal attendant

Marta…A Watcher

Carom…A Watcher from Mosshire

Jonah…A Watcher from Mesarra

Elsa…A Watcher at the Crystal Castle

Rogere…A Watcher at the Crystal Castle

Adele and **Jeremy**…the current Super Beings

Dr. Astarte…a Medical Doctor serving the royal court

Dr. Angelus…a Medical Doctor and Doctor of Magical Studies in Marinea

Commander Lockette...Leader of the newly-appointed Security Force

Amanda...Tamara's Social Secretary

Dana, Jon, and Borel...Members of the Security Force's Special Task Force

Shamous...Elf owner of **Your Every Wish**, a magical store

*   *   *   *   *

The Super Children

Solange...Tamara's grandmother and a Super Daughter/Sister, advisor to the King. Has silver hair and eyes like Marinean residents and wields white magic. Twin to Savea

Savea...Solange's twin and Super Daughter/Sister, living near a volcano. Has dark hair, skin and eyes unlike Marinean residents

Sostor...a Super Son/Brother/Twin and ice magic sorcerer on Mosshire. Ruler of the kingdom. Has fair skin, blonde hair and very blue eyes like residents of Mosshire

Sunan...a Super Son/Brother/Twin and solar magic mage on Mesarra. Ruler of the kingdom. Has dark hair and eyes like residents of Mesarra

Setting and Geography

Akura…the planet

Alteria…the land kingdom which succumbed to the Great Quakes. The remaining land portion is governed by a Council of Elders. Alterians have hazel eyes and blonde hair. No contact has been made with Marinea for generations.

Marinea…the kingdom under the sea formed after the Great Quakes divided the land kingdom of Alteria. Marineans have silver hair and eyes and are governed by a king. They have retractable gills in order to live on both land and sea.

Mosshire…a land kingdom in the cold north composed of small pieces of forested and ice-covered land joined by bridges, ruled by Sostor, an ice magic sorcerer. Residents have fair skin, blonde hair and very blue eyes.

Mesarra…a land kingdom in the south composed of a great desert. Residents are from tribes ruled by Sostor, a solar magic mage. Residents have very dark hair, skin and eyes.

Crystal Saga

7 - *Looking Forward . . .*
and Backward

D. E. Weingand

Prologue

My name is Trident and I am the former Prince, then King, of Marinea, an undersea kingdom created when Great Quakes caused much of Alteria to sink beneath the sea, leaving an island mainland behind. When I was Prince, I lived incognito on the Alteria mainland where I met my soon-to-be wife, Terra, when walking on the beach. It was one of the happiest times of my life. We became parents of two lovely daughters: Tamara, who was born with a crystal on her stomach and is now Queen and the present ruler of Marinea; and Trina, who has come of age and is excitedly exploring her newly-acquired powers.

After I was recalled to my undersea kingdom of Marinea due to the supposed death of my father, I lost track of time and was absorbed with being a good ruler. My wife and daughters continued to live on the mainland until the time of more quakes and a giant tsunami that brought the three of them to Marinea. Tamara was old enough to have developed gills; my mother, the Super Sister Solange, and I rescued my wife and younger daughter, Trina. Savea, twin Super Sister to Solange, had a falling out with her years ago after they both fell in love with my father. Tamara, using her powers, was able to heal this breach and now the Sisters are friends once again.

While I was still King, Terra, Trina and I were kidnapped from a Bubble Train and believed to be fatally injured in the apparent accident. The perpetrator was Sostor, the ice mage and ruler of the northern kingdom of Mosshire. We were eventually rescued by Tamara and the Super Sisters, who are two of the four Super Children created by the Super Beings with the permission of the Creator Being. The other two Children are male: Sostor (our kidnapper) and Sunan (solar mage and ruler of the kingdom of Mesarra in the south).

You may be wondering why I am no longer King. These tumultuous events prompted me to rethink my life choices and I decided to abdicate in order to spend precious time with my family. Tamara was next in line to the throne and was crowned Queen while her family was still being held captive in Mosshire. The questions that remain as to who was responsible and why the kidnapping took place are still under investigation.

Just before a planned tournament opened in Marinea, my wife, Terra, admitted to us that she was a Watcher, one of the magical beings that the Creator Being had put in place to monitor the activities of other beings. She was given the gift of an extended life span, but also the assurance that she could stay with us until our life spans ended. As a Watcher, she is not allowed to affect events, but only to observe and report back to the Creator Being.

I was going to move back to Alteria mainland with Terra and Trina when my mother, Solange, came up with an alternative suggestion. She asked me to consider living half-time on Alteria and half-time here as Special Councillor to the Queen. I was seriously considering that option when Trina asked if we couldn't just stay here. That possibility seemed to appeal to the whole family, so I agreed to do so.

Working with Tamara was the Commander, who she had appointed to head a new Security Force for the kingdom. The Commander had organized a Tournament of Martial Arts, which I mentioned earlier, with a two-fold purpose: as entertainment for our citizens and, perhaps more importantly, as a way to assess the competence of security forces from other kingdoms that were modeled after ours. Sadly, this turned out to be an unfortunate plan, as the athletes who attended were artificial beings—as were the vendors and booths that complemented the festivities. After this hoax was discovered, the Commander had the stadium evacuated—an excellent decision, as it exploded and disintegrated right after we all exited. More questions keep surfacing concerning who, what and why this hoax was designed and carried out.

We all met in the Commander's office to have a

debriefing about the hoax. It seemed that everyone was involved in some sort of new beginning. The future stretched out before us and we were eager to begin new adventures. As a father, I can't help being intrigued by the glances that occur between Tamara and the Commander. I suspect this may be another beginning.

Chapter 1
Beginnings Have Clues

Tamara and Trina were strolling in the garden. It was a lovely day and they could see dolphins frolicking outside the dome covering the kingdom. Tamara looked carefully at Trina's attire and asked about her blue cloak. Trina admitted that it still had not returned and was still a band around her waist.

"I don't understand it," she complained. "What possible danger could there be? Everything seems to be calm since the stadium exploded."

"How can you say that, Trina?" Tamara chided. "We haven't discovered any answers to our many questions. I don't know if that tournament fiasco was a one-time event—or a practice for something far larger."

"Apparently my cloak agrees with you," replied Trina." Did you bring your magic glasses with you?"

"Of course," Tamara answered. "I keep them on me at all times so I can check on my surroundings. One can't be too careful. Whoever designed that hoax is both powerful and clever."

"Tamara, look! Father's coming," cried Trina.

Tamara automatically put on her magic glasses that could look through spells. "Trina," she cautioned, "It looks like Father, but it's not! Be careful."

"Trident" approached the girls and called, "Good morning, my beautiful daughters! Trina, would you please do me a favor and take this package to the Commander's office?"

Tamara sent a mental message to the Commander urging him to come to her right away. Trina let her crystals know that she would like vines to secure this figure in front of her. Both things happened almost at the same time.

The Commander greeted Tamara and Trina and welcomed "Trident". He watched vines snake up the figure of Trident and hold him fast. "What is going on?" he asked.

Tamara answered, "I put my glasses on and saw that it was not Father. Trina had her crystals bind him in vines."

Trina added, "He wanted me to take that box to your office."

The Commander immediately cast a spell to isolate the box and it was just in time. A few minutes later, the box exploded.

Just then, the real Trident came out of the palace. He saw his image bound in vines and looked with surprise at Trina. "Would someone please explain this to me?"

Tamara once again related what had happened. "We need to figure out what is going on, Father. Trina's cloak is still not back, so our danger is still present."

Trident asked, "I heard an explosion. What was that?"

The Commander replied, "When I arrived, I cast an isolating spell around the box that the artificial you tried to get Trina to deliver to my office. Fortunately, the spell prevented the explosion from having any effect."

"I see," commented Trident. "So we have had artificial vendors and athletes, and now a replica of me. Do you have any clues as to why this is happening or who might be behind it?"

"Sadly, I do not—yet," replied the Commander. "But it does seem to me that someone is trying to harm our kingdom. The motive is unknown."

"But how does that someone know what Father looks like? It's a perfect likeness," asked Tamara.

"That's a good point," replied Trident. "I haven't been very visible since I was rescued from the kidnapping. I was present at the tournament, but artificial beings were already being used at that time. And before the tournament, I was held captive in Mosshire."

At that moment, Solange and Savea came rushing up. "We heard an explosion," Savea cried. "Is everyone all right?"

"Yes," responded Trina, "Thanks to Tamara and her magic glasses." She then brought the Sisters up-to-date on what had occurred. When she got to the part about Trident's double, Solange hugged her son in relief. "Grandma," asked Trina, "Do you have any idea how someone could have so accurately copied Father's appearance?"

"No," answered Solange.

"Yes," replied Savea. Everyone stared at Savea.

"What do you know?" queried the Commander.

"I don't 'know'," responded Savea. "It's more like a hunch. Solange, remember when Sunan was walking you through the five senses as a way to trigger your memories? He was focused on your wedding night. At no point did he ever try to stimulate memories of Trident's birth."

Solange confirmed, "That's true. But what's your point?"

"It's a suspicion that I have," Savea said. "Would you allow me to put you in a light relaxed state and take you back to when you gave birth?"

"Certainly. I trust you, Savea," agreed Solange.

Chapter 2
The Past is Present

Savea and Solange walked into the Private Dining Room from the garden and over to a couch along one wall. The others followed closely behind.

Once Solange was made comfortable and lying down, Savea raised her hands and a blue mist settled over her sister. Chanting softly, Savea then asked Solange to think about the day she went into labor with Trident. "Please describe the room you are in and anyone who was with you."

"I am in my bedroom and a doctor and nurse are with me. I don't know who they are. They are in medical clothing and are busy examining me and giving me instructions about breathing. Like my wedding night, I have a scarf tied around my eyes because it's 'tradition'," described Solange.

"Didn't you think that was strange?" asked Savea.

"I did," agreed Solange, "But the intensity of the pain grabbed my attention. Now the pains are increasing in frequency and I am being told to 'push'. I comply and then the pain subsides for a short time before building up again. I'm told to 'push' again and then the pain lessens once more. Once more

I'm told to 'push' and the pain is ended. I hear the doctor say that it's a boy before I'm given a shot and then I must have passed out.

"When I awaken, the doctor is gone and the nurse hands me my baby boy, all swaddled in a blue blanket. I felt such joy looking at his tiny face," Solange cooed. "And the scarf around your eyes was gone?" asked Savea. "Yes," said Solange.

"You may sit up now, Solange," instructed Savea. "By my count, you were told to 'push' three times and twice, the pain went away and then returned. Do you agree?"

"That's what I remember," Solange agreed.

"Did anyone in the room say anything else?" asked Savea.

"I did hear someone say 'once more'," Solange murmured "and then the baby cried." "How many times?" pressed Savea. "A couple of times," admitted Solange.

Trident sat next to his mother and put his arm around her shoulders. "I'm sorry I was so difficult, Mother." "Childbirth is not easy, Son," Solange reminded him, "But the outcome is worth all the effort."

"Now I'd like to share my suspicion with all of you," Savea insisted.

"I would be interested in hearing you as well," said Terra. "I have been observing your entire experiment. As a

Watcher, I have seen many births and have also given birth personally twice." Turning, she moved to sit next to her husband.

Savea continued, "I believe that Solange had twins."

The silence in the room was palpable. "I agree," said Terra. "The evidence is compelling."

"What evidence?" cried Solange.

Terra placed her hands on both Solange and Trident. "Solange, you were asked to do a push two times and then the pain abated. One more push and the pain ended. That is consistent with two births and an afterbirth. Plus, we need to acknowledge that the Super Children are actually two sets of twins because of the division. That genetically predisposes any pregnancies that come from them have a high probability of delivering twins."

Solange blanched, "And since we believe that one of the Super Brothers is Trident's father, Savea's belief seems credible! Oh my, if all this is true, what happened to the other babe?"

"There's one more possibility that I want to emphasize," said Savea. "Twins can be fraternal—not alike—or identical. If your twins are identical, the other twin would look just like Trident. We don't know who took the babe, or why. But if the babe was raised to be aware of Trident and to resent his success, then envy and jealousy could be a powerful motivator for bad behavior."

"This is making my head hurt," claimed Tamara. "I may have an unknown uncle who may be planning terrible things. How can we confirm these suspicions? And how can we confront possible future attacks?"

"My blue cloak can be a good indicator," offered Trina. "Until it assumes its original shape, we need to assume that we are all in danger."

"I agree," confirmed the Commander. "For now, let's move backward in time and think about who might have taken the child. My first instinct is to reexamine the Super Brothers. How can we revisit the time of the so-called cure of the imbalance? Is there some way to verify if that actually took place or was a sham to lead us astray?"

"I would like your permission," proposed Terra, "to ask the Creator Being to allow us to go back in time."

"Is that really possible?" asked Trident.

"Of course. The Creator Being can do anything," she answered. "But a second request is important. I would like to know if there was a Watcher monitoring that birth and what he or she observed. I will get back to you as soon as I can. In the meantime, it might be useful to imagine some scenarios that could explain some of these mysteries." Terra kissed Trident and hurriedly left the room.

Chapter 3
Creating Scenarios

After Terra left, there was silence in the room, except for some soft sobbing. Solange had her hands over her face and Trident was trying to comfort her. "Mother, none of this was your fault. You have been an unwitting victim from the very beginning. Personally, I'm stunned by the possibility that I have a twin brother who looks exactly like me and may have hostile intentions."

Savea went to sit beside Solange and held her hand. "I was reluctant to upset you, but I felt strongly that we needed to look at all potential threats, both past and present. Please let me know if I can do anything to make you feel better."

"I don't blame you for anything, Savea," assured Solange, squeezing Savea's hand. "Your suspicions may well be the key to solving a lot of our mysteries. I'm somewhat annoyed at myself for not even wondering about some of these events that you have so clearly targeted."

"Don't be annoyed, Grandmother," assured Tamara. "You were so intimately involved—and spelled in addition to everything that was happening to you. I think we were all pawns in an elaborate game. I'm impressed that you survived as well as you did."

"Thank you for your kind words, Tamara," replied Solange. "However, I think the time for rationalization is over. We must now begin to think assertively and seek concrete ideas about how to move forward. We are clearly under attack and have been for many years, without being aware of it."

"I agree, Solange," affirmed the Commander. "The time for taking the offensive is past due. We have all been shocked today. I recommend that we try to relax and gather our thoughts before reconvening tomorrow to create a series of scenarios. Let's meet here for breakfast and begin our discussion."

*   *   *   *   *

The next morning, one-by-one the planning group drifted into the Private Dining Room to have breakfast. It was evident that the Commander's directive to relax had not taken hold. Weariness hung like a cloud over the breakfast table. After trying to appreciate the expansive repast before them, Tamara asked the servers to clear the table and provide beakers of water for the discussion ahead.

The Commander entered and apologized for being late. He explained that he had needed to increase the security around the room to ensure privacy. Before the servers could finish readying the table for the meeting, he grabbed a plate and filled it with some nourishment for himself. *"I've done all I could with physical security. I strongly suggest that we communicate mentally during this meeting to assure that our ideas remain classified."* Everyone nodded agreement in support of his proposal.

"I am going to begin with one scenario," he began. *"After we are satisfied with it, we can begin another. This scenario is in strong support of Savea's suspicion. Two babes are born and are identical. The doctor is a sophisticated artificial being and takes one of the babes with him to give to the author of this plot.*

"We all know how Trident's life has developed; that is public knowledge. We do not know how the other twin grew up. For the sake of this scenario, I am going to suggest that he was raised in relative poverty, without loving parents. As he came of age, he was taken from that situation and placed in a school of magical studies. His innate magical skills were identified and additional skills taught until he was a magical prodigy. At that point, the author of this plot, who had been his mentor at the school, disclosed to him his true birth situation and nurtured his emerging resentment. How does this resonate with you so far?"

Everyone at the table stared at the Commander as he finished. Solange stood and began to pace the floor. *"What you* are suggesting sounds absolutely plausible," she asserted. "*I've been wrestling with designing a scenario all night and came up with nothing. I think you have it exactly right!*"

As they went around the table, the Commander's scenario was soundly approved and no other version was proposed.

Savea echoed Solange's support and commented that this outpouring was both impressive and a clear endorsement of moving forward with this scenario.

"*There is a clear gap in this scenario, however,*" Tamara insisted. "*We don't know who this 'mentor' was.*"

"*That's true,*" the Commander admitted. "I*'m hoping that when Terra returns, we may have a direction to pursue.*"

As if on cue, Terra entered the room and took a seat at the table. Smiling, she informed them that the Creator Being had granted both requests. She had permission to reverse time and, indeed, there was a Watcher present when Trident was born. It was the nurse who presided at the birth. "*The nurse has agreed to accompany us when we reverse time and explain what she observed,*" Terra said. "*When we undertake this journey, we will not be visible. Essentially, you will all become volunteer Watchers for the purpose of this endeavor.*"

The Commander asked, "*How many years will we be able to observe?*" He briefed her on the scenario that had

14

captured everyone's support and noted that it covered at least several decades.

"We will not be bound by the normal pace of time. We are allowed to accelerate or skip ahead at will," Terra informed them.

"That's amazing!" Trina chimed in. *"Am I allowed to go along?"*

"Of course, dear," Terra assured. *"You are an important part of this investigative team. Sleep well tonight, everyone. We leave after breakfast tomorrow."*

Chapter 4
Journey Through Time

The next day, after breakfast, the investigative team joined Terra and an unknown woman in the Private Dining Room. "This is Marta," she said, as she introduced another Watcher. "She was present at Trident's birth and can explain to us what we are seeing. We do not have to communicate mentally. Anything we speak will be known only to this group."

"Now," she continued, "In order to begin our journey, we need to hold hands and stay connected throughout. Do not let go or you may be stranded in that instant of time. Are there any questions?"

Trident asked, "Am I correct that we will go back in time to the time of my birth and then move forward in time? Will it be possible to revisit any portion of our journey or must the time progression always be forward?"

Terra replied, "You are correct and no, we cannot reverse time while in the midst of the journey. This is a one-time experience, so everyone should pay close attention."

"Can we halt the progression in order to ask questions

and communicate with each other?" asked Tamara.

"Yes, that is possible. As I am the leader of this time journey, please address all questions and requests to me," specified Terra. "Marta will be narrating what we see as we go along. If there are no other questions, please link hands and we shall begin. Remember that no-one can see you."

Terra waved her hands and a portal opened before them. Linking hands, as instructed, they entered the portal and found themselves in Solange's bedroom during her labor. Trina gasped as her blue cloak appeared around her. Terra smiled and said, "It makes sense that it has reappeared. We are in no danger here."

Marta began to narrate by explaining that Trident was about to be born. She pointed out that the artificial doctor had moved to the side and she was in charge of the actual delivery. Once she had received the babe, she cleaned him up and made sure that he had cried. Wrapping him in a blue blanket, she laid him in a bassinet next to the bed. Solange had relaxed and drifted off to sleep when her contractions started again. Urging Solange to push once more, she received a second babe and repeated the process of cleaning his airway and wrapping him in a blanket—this time, a green one. The "doctor" stepped forward, took the babe and left the room.

"Where did he take the babe?" Solange asked Terra.

Terra looked at Marta, who shrugged and did not answer. "Marta doesn't know. She had to tend to Solange, who was expelling the afterbirth."

"So that's an important piece of information that journeying back in time won't provide," concluded the Commander. Sadly, Terra agreed.

"But we do know that Solange definitely had twins," reminded Savea. "Yes, we do," affirmed Terra.

"Is there any way to follow that fake doctor and see where he goes?" asked the Commander.

"Let's try," offered Terra as she walked toward the door, leading the group into the hall. "Remember to keep holding hands," she said.

Spying the "doctor" at the end of the hall, she walked faster, urging the group to hurry. They watched him enter a door and close it behind him. As they reached that door, Terra stopped and said, "We can move through walls and doors because we are on an astral journey. Don't be afraid."

The group followed Terra through the closed door and into the room beyond. The "doctor" was handing the babe to a man seated behind a desk.

"Does anyone recognize that man?" demanded the Commander. Everyone answered negatively. The mysterious man thanked the "doctor" and left the room. The group hastened behind him, but he was too quick and exited the building to board a waiting car.

"Now what?" Solange asked Terra.

"I don't know," admitted Terra. "Marta, you were the designated Watcher on this case. Where did you pick up the trail?"

"We next found him when he was ten years old," she said. "He was homeless and living on the street. A local gang was trying to recruit him. He had learned slight of hand very well and was a talented thief. He had rejected the gang several times and appeared to be independent in his thievery. Once we had located him, he seemed to sense our presence and disappeared into a crowd. He definitely had innate magical skills and used them cleverly. We lost track of him again until he was about seventeen."

"When he was coming of age!" cried Tamara.

"Yes. And this is where the story becomes confused and complicated," added Marta.

Chapter 5
The Journey Continues

"Please explain," urged Savea.

"The Watcher in charge observed that when the boy came of age, a man stopped him in the street and offered to pay the tuition for him to enter an Academy of the Magical Arts. The boy apparently accepted the offer and the man and boy entered a nearby car," explained Marta. "The Watcher also had a car and followed them to the Academy. The Watcher remained on duty and reported that the boy not only took classes at the Academy, but also received housing and meals as well. This situation continued for several years. The man visited the boy regularly and they seemed to have a good relationship."

"Where was this Academy?" asked Tamara.

"Right here in Marinea," answered Marta.

"Here?" cried Tamara. "That's outrageous that a child could be living on the street in MY kingdom!"

"Tamara," soothed Solange. "Remember that you hadn't been born yet and when you were, you lived on the mainland with your parents."

"Then, one day, the man and boy left the Academy together and never returned," continued Marta. "The Watcher was unable to track where they went as he was frozen in place by a spell. By the time another Watcher released him, the pair was long gone," Marta reported sadly.

"Do we have a description of this mysterious man?" asked the Commander.

"That's another dilemma," admitted Marta. "The man's face was never in focus so the Watcher could not identify him."

"So the two of them are completely off the grid?" inquired Solange.

"I'm afraid so," Marta sighed. "The Watcher checked with the Academy, but all trace of the boy had been magically erased. Even his dorm room had been completely destroyed."

"How long ago did that occur?" asked the Commander. "Could we gain access to that dorm room?"

"Several years ago," replied Marta. "But the Academy has not repaired the room because of lack of funds."

"That's helpful," the Commander smiled. "Can you get us into that room?"

"I can," Marta said. "Keep holding hands while I do so."

*   *   *   *   *

In what seemed to be just a minute, the group was

standing in a room that had been completely demolished. Trident looked out the window and commented, "This is definitely in Marinea. I can recognize some of the buildings. I wasn't aware that there was an Academy of Magic in my kingdom."

"I was," said the Commander. "This is where I studied and earned my degree. The Academy keeps a low profile. By the time you became King, Trident, the Academy had transformed itself into a martial arts school, concealing its true purpose."

Tamara asked, "Commander, why did you bring us here? Do you have a way to find intel in what looks to be a war zone?"

"I'm going to try," responded the Commander. "While I was a student, some of us practiced various spells that would disguise our rooms so that they looked like something other than what they truly were—along the lines of what the Academy did on a larger scale. I want to try some of the reversal spells to see if anything is not as it looks."

"Solange, since we must continue to hold hands, may I enlist your help—your hand—in casting these spells?" inquired the Commander.

"Of course," she agreed.

He softly whispered each spell to her. Together, they

began to increase the volume to a full-body chant and a soft silver mist began to fill the room.

Gradually, the room began to shiver and morph into a more collegiate decor. There were books and papers on a table situated next to a comfortable looking bed.

"I was right!" exclaimed the Commander. "The boy was truly a magical prodigy and a master of disguise. Since we can't stop holding hands, is there a way to transport these books and papers, and anything else of interest, back to my office in our time?"

Marta looked at Terra, "What do you think?" she asked. Terra nodded agreement, chanted a short spell, and the entire contents of the room disappeared.

"I'm afraid your office will be quite crowded when you return, Commander. Even the bed was included!" laughed Terra.

Chapter 6
A Dead End

"Where shall we go next?" asked Trina. "We don't know where the mystery man took the boy."

"That's true," admitted Trident. "But perhaps when we go through what was just sent to the Commander's office, we will uncover some clues."

The Commander nodded, "I think we might. However, before we leave here, I recommend that we snoop around this building and see if we can overhear any conversation pertaining to the boy. It's great that we can't be seen, but the downside is that we can't question anyone."

"Remember that we must travel as a group," reminded Tamara. "Don't feel that you have to walk around people. We can walk right through them, as easily as through doors and walls."

Moving swiftly into the hall, the group spied some students lounging in a common area just ahead. Proceeding closer so that they could hear what the students were saying, they were pleasantly surprised that the boy was the chief topic of conversation. They were sharing stories of his antics as a student and the amazing feats of magic that he was able to produce.

Then they moved on to talk about the man who used to visit him regularly. No one seemed to know who that man was, but they often went on long walks together. Of particular interest to the Commander was the mention of the boy's sudden disappearance. One day he was a student comrade and the next day he was gone without a trace—and his dorm room was totally destroyed. There was only one thing left in the room: a bowl of sand.

"Yes!" cried the Commander. "We have a clue at last. The boy left a message behind."

"What clue?" asked Trina.

Savea smiled and said, "The sand."

*   *   *   *   *

Back in the Commander's office, the group was seated and sifting through the papers that had been found in the boy's dorm room. Tamara grew impatient with the slowness of their progress and threw up her hands. Everyone noticed that her bracelets had begun to glow. As they stared at her, the papers began to fly around the room and land in piles on the floor. A few of the piles also seemed to glow.

"What just happened?" asked Trident.

"I think my bracelets decided to help us," laughed

Tamara. "Let's focus on the glowing piles," she said, picking up one of the piles. "This pile consists of personal research about living in the desert," she related. "That seems consistent with the bowl of sand."

"And this pile is all about multiple births," added Solange.

"My pile goes further and analyzes abandonment issues," Terra said. "I think the mysterious man was priming the pump, so to speak, and leading the boy's curiosity in specific directions."

"My pile is much darker," mentioned the Commander. "The pages are written in a personal hand and itemize ideas for 'getting even' and strategies for revenge. Some of the latter are prototypes for what we experienced in the tournament."

"I'm seeing a pattern here," observed Marta. "That 'mysterious man' appears to be a puppet-master and a gifted one, at that. He led that boy down a preordained path that could only lead to a negative outcome. I don't believe the boy was inherently evil. I think he was essentially brainwashed into doing the man's bidding."

"How sad," sighed Solange as she watched Tamara walk across to where the books from the boy's room had been stacked. Stretching out her hands once again, Tamara watched her bracelets rearrange the books into stacks, some of which glowed.

"These books are about spells that create artificial beings and disguises," interpreted Tamara. "They certainly support the craziness that afflicted the tournament. I think our primary challenge is two-fold: 1) Identify and neutralize the 'mystery man'; and 2) Find the boy and figure out how to reverse the brainwashing that has occurred."

"Does anyone have any suggestions regarding how to begin?" asked the Commander.

Savea started, "We certainly can't ask Sunan to help. For all we know, he may be the 'mystery man'.

Terra asked Marta, "Do you know the identities of the Watchers in Mesarra?"

"I don't, but I can find out," she replied as she left the office.

"Wait!" called Solange. "Marta, please find out the names of the Watchers in Mosshire as well and invite all of the identified Watchers to join us for breakfast in the morning."

Nodding, Marta agreed to do so.

"What are you thinking, Mother?" asked Trident.

"I'm considering the possibility that all of these 'clues' could be disguises and misdirection," Solange responded. "We need to follow the clues, of course, but we should also go down the opposite paths and see where everything leads."

"Well-reasoned," approved the Commander. "You are a born leader."

Chapter 7
The Breakfast

The Private Dining Room was filled with both the investigative group and the invited guests from the Watcher community. After introductions had been made, Tamara formally welcomed the guests and asked for their assistance on an important matter. She asked her bracelets to enable mental communication in everyone in the room and asked them to use it.

Terra and Marta took turns relating the events of the journey. When they had finished, it was time for the Watchers from both Mosshire and Mesarra to share what they had witnessed over the same time period.

"Before we begin to hear from our guests," interrupted Trident, *"I'd like to pose an overarching question: Have you seen anyone who looks like me?"*

The Watcher guests looked shocked and huddled together, talking softly. The Watchers from Mesarra offered to begin. *"We have designated one Watcher from each group to summarize our observations. I am Jonah from Mesarra. We have been playing close attention to an apparent buildup of scientific and magical technologies. The factories involved have very tight security and little intel has been forthcoming. In response to your question, Trident, none of us have seen a being—real or artificial—who resembles you. Why do you ask?"*

"A boy who has reportedly come of age in the Academy of Magical Studies in Marinea has disappeared completely," replied Trident. *"A mysterious man visited him often while he was at the Academy and we don't know the identity of the man or where he was from. We believe that the boy is my twin, who we didn't know existed until quite recently. We have discovered that the boy is a magical prodigy and a master of disguise."*

"All of which suggests that the boy may NOT resemble Trident and has assumed a false persona, both physical and psychological," affirmed Savea. *"If so, it presents a significant challenge for you Watchers."*

"Indeed," agreed the designated Watcher from Mosshire. *"My name is Carom and I am pleased to help decode this puzzle. We have not detected any increase in technological development in Mosshire, but the security measures have been enhanced significantly. That makes us think that we are missing something in our observations. Given what Jonah has just reported from Mesarra, we must conclude that magic and disguise are definitely in play. We also have no intel about a*

being resembling you, Trident."

"So we now know a little about the two kingdoms, but nothing substantial," summarized Terra. *"Is there anything else you can share that might be useful to us?"*

Carom and Jonah consulted with their Watcher colleagues and then with each other. *"There is nothing else that would be helpful to you,"* Jonah reported. *"But we will all be on guard and get back to you with any more useful intel."* The Watcher guests then left the Private Dining Room to return to their normal duties.

"Now what?" asked Solange. *"We seem to be at a true dead end. I hate to admit it, but the boy in question has stymied us."*

"One thing is bothering me," noted Savea. "How old are you, Trident? We keep referring to your twin as 'the boy' and he is hardly that anymore."

"I'm somewhere in middle age," answered Trident. *"My age is difficult to determine because of my Super genealogy. That would also be true of my twin."*

"So we are no longer looking for a boy, but a full-grown man," asserted Tamara. *"Are there any other clues that could help identify him, even through disguises or magic?"*

"The glasses!" cried Trina. *"They would render any disguise or spell meaningless!"*

"*Of course!*" agreed Tamara. "*I had overlooked that very important asset. I think it is time for me to take the Brothers up on their invitations to visit their kingdoms. I would like one of the Sisters to accompany me while the other one helps Father govern Marinea. Your decision, of course.*"

"*I'm too close to this situation,*" admitted Solange, "*So I recommend that Savea travel with you. Is that acceptable, Savea?*"

"*Of course,*" Savea agreed. "*Tamara, let me know when the travel arrangements have been made.*"

"*Tamara, may I go with you?*" pleaded Trina. "*We could pretend that it is a vacation as well as a State Visit. I have a hunch that I could be an asset.*"

"*That's a good idea, Sis,*" replied Tamara. "*I agree with you and would welcome your assistance. After all, you are the second in line to the throne and should begin to learn about the other kingdoms.*"

"*What?!*" Trina squealed. "*I never thought about that! Oh my goodness, how my world is changing!*"

"*I will be sending the Security Task Force, under the command of Jon, with you,*" insisted the Commander. "*They will be dressed appropriately, but out of uniform.*"

"*Thank you, Commander,*" responded Tamara. "*You truly think of everything,*" she smiled.

34

Chapter 8
Official State Visits

A few days later, Tamara and her entourage boarded the Bubble Train to the mainland of Alteria. She intended to stop there for a few days to arrange for a system of diplomatic exchanges. When that part to the visit had been concluded, they boarded a private plane to take them to Mesarra. Stopping there first was her preference since Sunan had been so welcoming during his visit to Marinea.

She was taking no chances and intended to wear the "magic glasses" at all times during the trip. When the plane landed at the airport in Mesarra, she was surprised that Sunan himself was there to greet them. Her glasses affirmed that everyone in the welcoming party was real, which was a relief.

Sunan had provided enough transportation to accommodate the entire group, Tamara was fascinated that the vehicles were a combination of motorized transport and dune buggies. *"Of course,"* she thought, *"That makes sense since the kingdom is primarily a desert."*

Sunan, Tamara, Savea and Trina entered the first vehicle, accompanied by Jon and two members of the Security

Task Force. The other Task Force members rode in following vehicles with representatives from Mesarra. As the motorcade left the airport, Sunan provided commentary describing what they were observing. As expected, sand dunes were everywhere, but oases filled with palm trees, flowers and fountains were frequently seen.

"Your kingdom is beautiful," praised Tamara as they drove along. "I have heard rumors of increasing efforts to produce magical and technological products. Are those rumors true and, if so, might we have a tour of those facilities?"

"The security surrounding those installations is intense, but I could escort you and your companions in this car through one of them if you wish," suggested Sunan. "The other members of your party would have to meet us at the hotel after the tour."

Tamara agreed to those conditions and her vehicle sped away from the motorcade after informing the others of the change in plans. Since they no longer travelled on the main highway, the ride became quite bumpy. The detour was most informative to Tamara. Her glasses detected anomalies in the terrain. As she viewed the passing scenery, numerous oases appeared but the glasses revealed that only dunes were truly there.

Soon they arrived at what appeared to be a modern

factory building surrounded by lovely palm trees and flowers. However, the glasses showed a grim looking structure guarded by a large number of soldiers. As they walked toward the factory, each soldier "became" a palm tree when the glasses were not employed.

When they entered the building, they saw many employees working at an assembly line resulting in smart toys. Tamara adjusted her glasses to reveal that the 'toys' were actually smart weapons being constructed by 'employees' that were robots. Shocked, Tamara pretended to be fascinated by the 'toys' and complimented Sunan on his interesting factory.

At the end of the tour, Sunan escorted his guests back to the vehicle and they proceeded to the hotel. When they had checked into their rooms, Tamara asked that all members of her team come to her room for a short meeting. After all had assembled, she indicated that mental communication should be used, as she assumed that listening devices would be in place.

She briefly described out loud what they had all "seen"—and then switched to telepathy to inform them of what the glasses had revealed as truly there. Cautioning everyone to hide their shock, she switched back to speaking out loud as she sent everyone to their rooms to prepare for dinner.

*   *   *   *   *

At dinner that evening, they were entertained by singers

and dancers introduced as being from the local culture. Tamara was disappointed when her glasses identified the entertainers as artificial, probably androids. She wondered if there would be any opportunity to meet with the real citizens of the kingdom. Even the servers were artificial beings.

Sunan appeared to be a genial host and wine flowed liberally. Professing fatigue, Tamara requested an early night and asked her team to meet for another short meeting before retiring for the night. She also thanked Sunan profusely for his hospitality and mentioned that they had an early departure in the morning. He looked surprised at the brevity of the visit, but said he understood that the affairs of state often outweighed personal wishes.

In Tamara's room, she once again switched to telepathy and informed the team what her glasses had observed during the dinner. Trina added to her sister's haste to leave by remarking that her blue cloak had once again become a waist band, indicating the presence of danger. Tamara wished her team a good night's rest, but cautioned that they be alert to any danger.

*   *   *   *   *

In the morning, the team assembled for a joint breakfast and then took the motorcade to the airport. Jon and the Task Force carefully inspected the plane and removed both listening devices and suspicious—and possibly explosive—packages. When Jon was satisfied, they began to taxi down the runway.

Savea asked Tamara if she could borrow the glasses and put them on. She walked carefully down the aisle and opened the cockpit door. Looking at the pilot, she stopped abruptly and called silently to Jon. He came immediately to her side and she silently asked him if he could fly the plane. He said he could and she cast a spell on the pilot that immobilized him. Jon took the co-pilot's seat and gained control of the plane. Tamara joined them in the cockpit and Savea handed the glasses back to her, indicating that she should put them on. She complied and gasped. The pilot looked like her father!

*   *   *   *   *

As the plane approached the airport in Alteria, Tamara sent a message to Mosshire postponing her visit and citing a pressing need to return to Marinea. As they deplaned, a specially commissioned motorcade arrived to take them to a security-enhanced Bubble Train. Savea had added more spells to keep the prisoner restrained.

When they reached the Bubble Train, they boarded a car that had been especially designed to be escape-proof. The return trip to Marinea was uneventful and they were greeted at the station by the Commander and the rest of the Security Force, who were waiting to take the prisoner into custody.

Once he was placed in a special cell that had been designed to hold him safely, Tamara and the group adjourned to the Commander's office to discuss what had occurred on the journey and to plan for the future.

Chapter 9
Coming to Terms

Solange and Trident joined the group in the Commander's office. Solange's face looked strained and worried. *"I understand that we have my other son in custody,"* she began. *"Has anyone spoken to him?"*

"No," answered Tamara. *"Savea had to use spells to restrain him and they prevented any type of communication."*

"So what do we do now?" asked Trident. *"Can we see my brother?"*

"When you do," urged Tamara, *"Please take my glasses with you so he cannot confuse you with magic and disguise."*

"That's a good idea," affirmed the Commander. *"Remember that he is a master of the magical arts and you are just learning to explore your gifts, Trident. Plus, he may be harboring deep resentment of you and what he views as a life full of privilege and good fortune that he was entitled to and denied."*

"How can we convince him that we never knew he existed?" cried Solange in despair.

"I don't know," sighed Savea. *"He's had so many years*

to build up that resentment and blame us for his lot in life. And that mystery man, who is as yet unidentified, undoubtedly stoked that negativity. My only suggestion is to let Tamara speak with him. After all, she removed the ill will between us, Solange. Perhaps her bracelets can help in this situation as well."

Tamara looked stunned. *"My bracelets have always led me; I haven't led them. I don't know how they would react."*

"Please, Tamara, won't you just try?" pleaded Solange.

"I'll go with you, Sis," offered Trina, *"My blue cloak will let me know if we are in any danger. We can tell him the truth—that we have just learned that we are his nieces and would like to welcome him to our home. His magical skills should be able to recognize that we are being truthful—and I think it will be helpful that you are the ruler of Marinea, not his twin."*

"Those are good points, Trina," admitted Tamara. *"I can work with them. Commander, when can we visit the prisoner?"*

"I would like him to contemplate his fate until tomorrow," advised the Commander. *"After breakfast, I will accompany you to his cell."*

*   *   *   *   *

The next morning, the Commander escorted Tamara

and Trina to the magically enhanced cell containing the prisoner. Inside the cell, the prisoner stood glaring at them with malice in his eyes. "Why am I confined to this cell," he demanded to know. "And where exactly am I?"

The Commander replied, "You are in the kingdom of Marinea, an undersea kingdom ruled by Queen Tamara." Pointing to Tamara, he continued, "This is the Queen and she has come, with her sister, to welcome you to Marinea."

"Welcome me?" spat the prisoner. "Is this how you welcome all visitors to your kingdom?"

"Hardly," Tamara responded. "Only the ones who have hostile intentions toward us. You were posing as the pilot of the plane that was to take us home from Mesarra—a plane that was filled with listening and explosive devices. In addition, you were in disguise, hiding your true identity."

"I was following orders, nothing more," maintained the prisoner.

"Whose orders?" asked the Commander.

Hearing only silence from the prisoner, Trina jumped in, "What is your name? What can we call you? I'm Trina."

"You can call me X47," the prisoner growled.

That response prompted Tamara to put on her glasses. Gasping, she said, "That is the truth. But the truth also reveals that this is an android, not real. I don't know why the glasses didn't show me this before."

"Perhaps they only peel off one layer of deception at a time," offered Trina.

"If that is their purpose, then how are we to know when we are seeing the entire truth?" pondered Tamara. "Perhaps when we look again and nothing further has changed?"

"How many of you are there?" asked the Commander.

"As many as are required," muttered the prisoner.

"Where is the original being that is the model for replication?" demanded Tamara, as she cast a truth spell.

The prisoner squirmed and whispered, "Under house arrest" as smoke began to ooze from his body.

"He's self-destructing! Stand back!" urged the Commander.

*   *   *   *   *

As the smoke gradually cleared, the cell block was filled with prone bodies on the floor. Gradually, they stirred and began to sit up.

"Is anyone hurt?" asked the Commander. One by one, they assured him that they were fine—just stunned.

"So we have good news and bad news," summarized Tamara. "The bad news is that we didn't capture Trident's twin. The good news is that his twin did not participate voluntarily in the attacks during the tournament and our journey. He is being held captive, location unknown."

"There is one more piece of good news," added Trina. "Now that the android has blown himself up, my blue cloak has returned. The immediate danger is past."

Chapter 10
The Journey Resumed

Back in the Commander's office, the group began strategizing once again. "We are at a temporary dead end," the Commander decided.

"That's true," agreed Tamara, "but it gives us the opportunity to resume our journey. "If everyone is for it, I will contact Mosshire once again and get our journey back on track."

"I think it will be very useful to scout out Sostor's kingdom," said Savea. "Right now, it sure looks like Sunan is the mastermind behind these lethal shenanigans. But one can't be certain until all the evidence is in."

"Then if no one has any objections, as soon as Tamara has the trip to Mosshire confirmed, I will contact you with our itinerary," assured the Commander.

*   *   *   *   *

A few days later, the Commander contacted the members of the team and distributed the promised itinerary. The next morning, they would be taking the Bubble Train to Alteria, as before, and then boarding a private jet to Mosshire.

He had briefly considered reentering the tunnel that had been created to rescue Tamara's family, but decided to hold that idea in reserve. Since this was to be a State Visit, using a private jet was a reasonable means of travel. They would be beginning the journey in the morning.

In the meantime, he perused all available intel about the kingdom of Mosshire. Tamara had informed him that they would be housed in a comfortable hotel near the palace. A formal reception had been organized for the evening after their arrival. All ambassadors in residence had been invited; it was to be a very fancy affair. The following day, a tour of the kingdom was scheduled.

The Commander read and reread the intel until the words appeared blurry. He was concerned about the lack of detail and hard data. Sostor's paranoia about security was clearly evident. He decided to set up an urgent meeting with Jon and the Security Task Force to discuss possible issues that they might confront.

*   *   *   *   *

The next morning, the team boarded the Bubble Train and began the journey. Everything proceeded smoothly and they were soon airborne enroute to Mosshire. Once they landed, a motorcade awaited to take them to the designated hotel. They were pleasantly surprised to find delicious meals waiting in their rooms. After a rest period, they began to dress for the formal reception.

Tamara had brought a lovely sea blue dress made of a material that didn't seem to wrinkle; it was encrusted with dolphins made of seed pearls. A matching pearl tiara announced her rank. A young woman had been assigned as a personal assistant while she was in Mosshire and was very helpful in getting her ready for the event.

Savea had been assigned an adjoining room, which made Tamara feel much safer. On the other side of Tamara's room, Terra and Trina shared a room. The Security Task Force members of the team were just down the hall.

At the designated hour, the entire team made their way to the palace to attend the reception. Sostor greeted them at the entrance to a large Ballroom. He offered his arm to Tamara and led her inside.

Trina took Jon's arm and followed closely behind. Her blue cloak had once again compressed to a waistband, indicating danger and she wore the magic glasses as a precaution. She was wearing a green outfit designed to appear as a dress, but was actually loose pants that allowed her to kick.

Terra and Savea entered together, followed by the Task Force members, who separated as soon as they were inside in order to observe the entire area.

The room was filled with dignitaries and other invited guests. Staff holding trays filled with delicacies and glasses of various drinks circulated throughout the room. Tamara looked around with interest and asked Sostor to introduce her to some of the attendees.

Trina was the first to sound a mental alarm. She had put on the glasses as soon as she entered and started to scan the room. The first thing she noticed was the potted palms arranged around the perimeter. Gasping, she realized that the palms were actually artificial soldiers holding weapons. Looking more deeply at the guests, it became obvious to her that no one in the room was real—except for the members of her team. She next focused her attention on Sostor to find that he, also, was an artificial being.

Sending an urgent mental message to Tamara, she transmitted all her findings and asked what they could do to get out of there. Tamara responded that she would pretend to faint and the entire team should come to take her back to the hotel. Trina sent a mental SOS to the team and they all came to her side. Tamara proceeded to 'faint' and the entire team rushed to her, gently lifting her and heading for the door. Suddenly the doors slammed shut and were blocked by the faux palm trees. Trina extended her arms toward the doors and the crystals on her hands blew a hole through which they could escape.

Once outside, Tamara regained her footing and ordered the team to head toward the nearby beach. She erected a magical barrier behind them and joined the team as they entered the water. She gave a second order to move as quickly as possible to the now closed entrance to the lava tunnel that had been created to rescue her family. Mentally, Trina contacted the Commander and asked that he and the Security Force meet them in the tunnel.

As they neared the closed tunnel entrance, Savea sent a ray of power toward it, opening it so they could enter easily. They could hear the sound of pursuit behind them; apparently, the artificial beings had broken through Tamara's makeshift barrier.

"Quickly," she urged the team to move into the tunnel. Once they were all inside, she once again closed that entrance so the pursuers were blocked.

They raced through the tunnel as fast as they could go, stopping only to catch their breaths when necessary. After they could no longer hear the sounds of pursuit, Tamara halted their progress and created a special spell that would increase the speed of their forward movement. The distance to the kingdom of Marinea was great, but the spell made it feel insignificant—especially when they could see the Commander and the Security Force coming toward them. Tamara added a spurt of energy and collapsed into the Commander's arms.

*　　*　　*　　*　　*

Solange and Trident met the team at the entrance to the tunnel in Marinea. Savea asked her sister to help her place additional traps and barriers in the tunnel so that an invasion could not be successful. The exhausted team entered the airlock and reconvened on the Practice Field.

The Commander helped Tamara to a nearby chair and asked for a summary of their experiences in Mosshire. Trina stepped forward and twirled so that her now restored cloak swirled around her. "At least now," she crowed, "my cloak has become normal once again. All the time in Mosshire, it was just wrapped around my waist. It wasn't until I put on the glasses at the so-called reception that I could see the truth of our situation."

An exhausted Tamara shared her frustrations, "I thought that Sostor was being hospitable when he met us at the door to the Ballroom. I can't believe that I did not detect the falseness of his persona. Now we have an additional puzzle to decode: where is the real Sostor?"

Chapter 11
Finding Sostor

After a night of rest and enjoying a delicious breakfast, Tamara requested a meeting with the Commander. He scheduled the Private Dining Room for the meeting since he believed that the entire team—plus Solange and Trident—should be present. Once everyone had arrived, he requested that everyone participate in revisiting the details of their harrowing journey, and to communicate mentally.

Tamara began, *"I had no idea that this would be other than a typical State Visit. It is too bad that we could not experience the tour that was scheduled for today. I wonder what they are concealing?"*

"I find the most curious question to be: where is Sostor?" interjected the Commander. *"Has he been captured or worse—and, if so, by whom? I don't see any reason for a replica to be in place."*

"It's hard not to invent conspiracy theories at this point," offered Savea. *"Trident, you are a talented politician. Do you have any insights as to what is going on in Mosshire? Your experience there as a captive may suggest something."*

"*As I think back on it, I am doubting everything I thought I knew,*" Trident responded. "*If Tamara could not detect that the Sostor she just met was false, then what about me? Was the Sostor who kidnapped me real or false? Was the Sostor who visited this kingdom for her birthday ball real or false? I think we have to question all of our previous assumptions.*"

"*One more thing,*" added Solange. "*What about the imbalance that Tamara supposedly healed in the Brothers? If Sostor was false, there was nothing to heal and the whole thing was a masquerade.*"

"*And as a Watcher,*" Terra chimed in, "*how much of what I have been observing and reporting was legitimate? Or have I been part of the game as well?*"

"*My head is starting to hurt again,*" complained Tamara. "*What do you think about another astral journey? Shall I go back to Mosshire and snoop around?*"

"*That may be the best way to get at the truth,*" admitted Terra. "*Meanwhile, I plan to get in touch with my colleagues on Mosshire and share what we have discovered.*"

"*Sis, can you take the glasses with you?*" asked Trina. "*I don't think so,*" answered Tamara, "*as my physical body will remain in my bed. Besides, I have a feeling that you may need them to see through disguises right here in Marinea.*"

Tomorrow, my next astral journey shall begin."

*   *   *   *   *

Tamara woke up early the next day. She was both eager to begin her astral journey and anxious about what it might reveal. Having asked for breakfast to be delivered to her bedroom, she waited for Mia's knock at the door. Hearing nothing, she walked to the door and looked out. She called Mia's name softly and was pleased to see her coming down the hall carrying a tray.

"I'm so glad to see you," Tamara called. "I want to fortify myself before beginning my journey." Mia stepped into Tamara's room and arranged the breakfast on a small table. "I'm not surprised," commented Mia. "Please be careful today."

"I'll do my best, Mia," Tamara agreed as she began to devour her breakfast. "Please lock my door on your way out so that I won't be disturbed during my journey." Mia nodded and left the room.

Having finished eating, Tamara returned to her bed and began to enter a state of relaxation.

*   *   *   *   *

Sinking into a sleep mode, she watched her bracelets begin to glow. Her eyes closed and she felt her astral self lift off the bed. She asked her bracelets to take her to Sostor and began the flight portion of her journey. Expecting to begin feeling cold, she was surprised to see the dunes of Mesarra appear in the distance. *"How interesting,"* she thought. *"But my bracelets are never mistaken."*

Her movement slowed and she landed in an oasis that looked unoccupied. Reaching into her pocket for a tissue, her hand brought out the magic glasses. *"That sister of mine,"* she giggled. *"She figured out how to include the glasses on my journey!"* Putting them on, she discovered that the oasis was not empty, but filled with robot guards surrounding a structure that was not visible before she donned the glasses. Hoping that the invisibility she enjoyed on her previous journeys still held, she walked closer to the structure.

Ignoring the heavily guarded door, she entered through a wall and found herself looking at Sostor. Removing the glasses for a moment, she watched the image of Sostor disappear. Replacing the glasses, she decided to watch and wait.

*   *   *   *   *

She didn't have long to wait. A short time later, Sunan entered through the guarded door. "Hello, Brother," said Sunan. "How are you today?"

"How do you expect me to answer that question?" responded Sostor. "This is the second time that you have captured me and drained my magic. By the way, how do you manage to do that?"

"That's a secret that I do not choose to share, Brother," answered Sunan. "You are a valuable source of magic that I can tap at will—and I intend to do so for a long time. I hope you are comfortable here and that your accommodations are satisfactory. After all, this is your home now."

Tamara had to cover her mouth so that her gasp could not be heard. She had not anticipated this development and could hardly believe what she was hearing. Her instinct was to end this journey and return home, but something was telling her to keep watching.

"Tell me, 'Brother'," sneered Sostor, "How many replicas of me have you made? And did you send me to the tournament?"

"I make as many as I need," laughed Sunan. "It's so easy to cloak you in evil and send you forth. It really amuses me. I could never have done it without the extra power that I drain from you. Your replicas are completely undetectable from the real you. That woman who thinks she's a queen tried to correct the imbalance between us—an impossibility to do when one of the parties is a replica! And to top it all off, she thinks I'M her grandfather!!! Isn't that a hoot?!"

"I fail to see the humor in any of that," challenged

Sostor. "She's a lovely girl and I'm proud of her."

Tamara shivered as the words sunk in. *"How are we ever going to defeat this monster?"* she wondered. *"He's so incredibly dangerous!"* A wave of shame swept through her as she realized how naive she had been to trust Sunan in the past. Then a second wave of determination and outrage helped her to focus on the future and an action agenda.

"But I'm not going to be naive again," she thought, making a commitment to not rush to judgment. She settled back to continue watching and waiting.

Once Sunan had left, she noticed that Sostor was looking right at her. Puzzled, since she knew that she couldn't be seen, she remained motionless and quiet. "I know that you are there, Tamara," accused Sostor. "Did you really think that you could fool us? Our combined power is significant and we can sense when you are present."

Sunan burst into the room and stood next to Sostor. "So our little charade didn't work?" he asked.

"I'm afraid not," answered Sostor. "We must eliminate her."

Tamara's arms rose automatically and created a barrier. Suddenly, she was back in her bed and safe—at least for the moment.

Chapter 12
New Twists

Tamara rang for Mia as soon as she was fully awake. "Mia, please send for the Commander, the Sisters, my parents, Jon and Trina. I need to speak to all of them immediately," she ordered.

After she had freshened up, she dressed for the day and waited for the team to arrive. The Commander came first, knocking softly and entering quickly. He walked over to her and put his arms around her. "Are you all right?" he asked with concern in his voice.

"Physically, yes—so far—and mentally in turmoil," she responded. *"We must use telepathy to communicate. I'll explain everything as soon as the others are here,"* she added, resting her head on his shoulder. His arms tightened around her and he placed a kiss on the top of her head. They walked together over to a couch and sat down.

"You weren't gone very long," he observed. *"Has something happened?"* Just then there were additional knocks at the door and the rest of the team entered. Tamara raised her arms and more chairs appeared so that everyone could be

seated.

"You look pale," Terra observed. "How are you feeling?"

Tamara reminded everyone to use telepathy and then continued, "*After I share my journey with you, you may all feel ill and look pale.*" She then described her experiences in detail, ending with, "*I fully expect an attack at any moment. We have no time to lose in preparing the kingdom.*"

"*I almost want to chuckle,*" commented Solange. "*Here we were, trusting Sunan, wondering who was Trident's father, and—in reality—we still don't know the answer to that question. And the truth lies somewhere in-between. Both Brothers are corrupted and the local Watchers either missed it or were complicit!*"

Terra looked at Tamara and asked, "*Are you certain that the Sostor you saw was real and not another replica?*"

"*I am,*" answered Tamara. "*Trina had slipped the glasses into my pocket and when I found them, I put them on immediately, discovered the building and walked inside. Seeing Sostor, I briefly removed them and he disappeared; then I put them on again and there he was. So it had to have been him.*"

"*I'm sorry, but I have to leave. I'll return as soon as I can,*" said Terra as she hurried out the door.

"What was that all about?" asked Trident.

"You know she's a Watcher, Father," explained Tamara. *"She has to report all this to the Creator Being immediately."*

"Of course," Trident admitted. *"I had quite fallen back into viewing her as my wife and your mother. So dealing with my captured replica is not at the top of our list anymore, is it?"*

"I'm afraid not," emphasized the Commander. *"I agree with Tamara that an invasion is imminent. She is their primary target and we must protect her at all costs."*

Savea smiled, *"I rather think that she will be protecting the rest of us, Commander."*

"No doubt, but we must be prepared nonetheless," he responded. *"Jon, please activate the entire Security Force and place us on Red Alert. Tamara, do you have any insight into their plans for an attack?"*

"I'm sorry, but I don't. I felt very threatened and aborted the journey immediately," she admitted. *"I'm afraid I don't have any further intel to share with you."*

"Our defenses are strong," said Savea, *"but I wish we had some way to learn what they are up to."*

"I'm going to send my spy birds back to Mosshirre and Mesarra on surveillance runs," decided the Commander. *"Perhaps they will discover something that will help us."*

"*And if they don't?*" asked Trident.

"*Let's take this one step at a time,*" suggested the Commander, as Terra burst through the door and hurried to join the group.

"*Mother, you look upset. What did the Creator Being tell you?*" asked Tamara.

"*The Watchers from both kingdoms are being recalled for interrogation,*" Terra answered. "*We shall soon know whether they were incompetent or complicit. Meanwhile, new crews of Watchers are being assigned to those locations.*"

"*What about the Brothers?*" asked Trident. "*We are expecting some kind of attack shortly.*"

"*The Creator Being has granted you some time. The progression of Time in the two kingdoms has been frozen until the fate of the former Watchers has been decided,*" responded Terra. "*But there is another piece of this puzzle that has surfaced. I have been informed that neither Brother is your father, Trident .*"

"*How can that be?*" cried Solange. "*We were so certain!*"

"*Do you remember that guard who was sprinkling glitter over the royal party on your wedding night during the storm, whenever they appeared to lose focus?*" Terra prompted.

Savea answered immediately, "*Of course. He was the only one who appeared to be real.*"

"*And he was the one who tied the scarf over my eyes,*" added Solange.

"*I've learned that he was a Watcher,*" Terra informed them. "*He was undercover at the time and his mission was to observe the two kings, past and present. The glitter was a subtle ploy to stay close to them.*"

"*So what are you trying to say, Mother?*" asked Tamara.

"*His mission brought him into contact with Solange,*" Terra explained. "*He was increasingly concerned for her safety and well-being. Over time, his concern grew into an emotional connection. When he observed the callousness of how she was being treated, his neutrality weakened and he intervened.*"

"*Are you saying that he was the lover in my bedchamber that night and the nights following?*" asked Solange.

"*Yes,*" revealed Terra. "*Eventually, he was discovered and reassigned.*"

"*Do you know where he is now?*" asked Solange.

"*I was not given that information,*" responded Terra. "*I am allowed to tell you that he was not punished, as his intentions were pure.*"

"*But why did he visit me only when I was fertile?*" wondered Solange.

"My instincts tell me that he knew, from observing the kings, that they would leave you alone once you were with child," suggested Terra.

"My goodness," breathed Solange, *"I am actually relieved. At my core, I wasn't comfortable with either Brother being Trident's father. But I have to admit that I am curious about the guard and his whereabouts."*

"There's another aspect of this revelation that we haven't considered," prompted Savea. *"The Watchers are magical beings. The mating of Trident and Terra was important to the amount of power received by their daughters. Now that we know the identity of Trident's father, your mating with him would have significantly affected the powers received by Trident—which, I think, we can assume to be substantial."*

"I agree, and it certainly explains the amazing range of Tamara's crystals," said Terra. *"We must increase our attention to that probability. Trident needs to be fully in control of his powers if we are to defeat the Brothers."*

Chapter 13
Understanding Trident

Tamara's head was spinning after all the new revelations. She fully understood her grandmother's reaction to the news, as she also had not been comfortable with the idea of having one of the Brothers as a grandfather.

Now she was mentally wrestling with the challenge of how to identify and control her father's presumptive powers. One by one, an idea would occur to her and subsequently be rejected. A knock at her bedroom door interrupted her reverie.

"Enter," she called.

The Commander opened the door and walked across the room to where she stood. Putting his arms around her, he asked if he could be of service. She sighed and gratefully lay her head on his chest. They moved together to sit on a nearby couch.

"Do you have any suggestions as to how we might learn about father's powers," she mentally asked. *"The Sisters were so helpful to me when I tried to figure out what my crystals could do."*

"I would recommend inviting them to help with this project as well," he said. *"After all, Solange is Trident's mother*

and definitely has a vested interest. And Savea has been bringing up very salient points; her insights are admirable."

"Those are good points," agreed Tamara. "Plus, their influence is considerable and I believe Father would be amenable to their directives. I would like you to be part of this effort, if you would be comfortable doing so. Your magical background would be an asset."

"Of course," he promised. "I'll help in any way that would be useful."

*   *   *   *   *

The next morning, Tamara invited the Sisters, the Commander and her family to join her on the boat for breakfast. After enjoying crab cakes and seaweed biscuits, they agreed to don the bubble headgear prior to a serious discussion.

Tamara activated her music device and said, *"I have to admit that I don't know where to start. Our goal is to help Father to discover and use his magic. Does anyone have any idea of where to start?"*

Savea proposed, *"We had good results with understanding your emerging powers, Tamara. We can try those approaches with Trident, beginning with the blue rays that he was able to utilize in Mosshire."*

"I'm comfortable with that," agreed Trident. *"What should we do first?"*

"*Do you see that log floating in the water over there? Blow it up,*" instructed Savea.

"*I see it, but how do I do that?*" asked Trident.

Tamara advised, "*Mentally see it explode.*"

Trident extended his hands toward the floating log and closed his eyes. The log flew toward the opposite shore.

"*Well, that's a beginning,*" laughed Savea.

Doubled over with giggles, Tamara asked, "*Father, did you think about it exploding or flying?*"

Trident looked at her sheepishly, "*I guess I didn't want it to blow up and pollute the water.*"

Terra suggested, "*Pretend it's a robot warrior and try again.*"

Trident extended his arms and thought about the robots at Mosshire. Blue rays shot across the water and the log burst into sawdust. "*I did it!*" he exclaimed.

"*I want you to try something, Son,*" said Solange. "*Mentally see that sawdust re-form into a log.*"

Trident gazed out at the sawdust floating on the water and extended his arms. Squinting, he sent a blue cloud over the sawdust, and gradually the dust became a log again.

"*Wow!*" cried Trina. "*That was awesome!*"

Terra kissed Trident and then applauded. "*That was magnificent! You have creation powers!*"

The entire group stared at Trident in awe.

"*Father, your powers are impressive!*" Tamara added with pleasure. "*It will be so much fun to explore them. Sadly, I believe we must do so with urgency since the potential invasion looms ahead.*"

"*Remember,*" the Commander reminded her, "*Terra said that Time has been frozen in the kingdoms ruled by the Brothers. That gives us some valuable latitude in this endeavor. How should we proceed now?*"

"*Since Savea and I have experience helping Tamara, I think we would be the logical ones to work closely with my son to explore his magic,*" offered Solange. "*Trident, is that acceptable to you?*"

"*Of course,*" he agreed. "*But I would like to add my daughters to this effort. I believe that Terra should not participate since she is bound by Watcher rules.*" Terra nodded and let the others know that she would be leaving to make a report to the Creator Being as soon as they returned to land.

The boat slowly turned and made its way to the dock. Trident suggested that his 'help team' join him for lunch and a planning session. Tamara ordered that telepathy be used at all times.

*   *   *   *   *

After lunch in the Private Dining Room, the 'help team'

and Trident decided to relocate to the Chapel for planning and practice. The Sisters began the session by asking Trident to light and extinguish candles, followed by moving objects across the room. He was able to do these tasks successfully.

Tamara then asked him if his body had changed in any way. He responded, *"When I was being held captive in Mosshire, I noticed that I could hear voices clearly that were very far away. I was puzzled by this."*

"And yet," she wondered, *"when I was talking mentally to Trina on my astral journey, you were not able to be part of the conversation."*

"I have to admit," he said, *"that I did hear you, but I had been beaten and I thought I was imagining it."* Tamara put her arms around her father and hugged him tightly. *"I'm so sorry, Father,"* she responded, *"I wish I had known."*

"Father," inquired Trina, *"has anything else about your physical capabilities changed?"*

"I'm not sure," he answered. *"I've never really thought about it. Can you help me figure it out?"*

Trina thought a moment and then offered, *"One thing that I've noticed about myself is that I have the ability to leap high and far. Can you do that?"*

"I don't know. Let me try," he said as he walked to the end of the aisle and started to run back toward her. He soared

into the air and landed on top of the altar. *"I guess I can!"* he crowed.

Solange walked over to Trident and helped him down from the altar. She guided him to a nearby couch and held his hand as she asked, *"Son, you've been through so much since your kidnapping that I wonder if you are fully aware of the many abilities your daughters have acquired since then. Let me summarize them for you:*

- *Tamara was born with one crystal on her stomach but, since she came of age, she has accumulated more crystals that seem to respond to her needs.*

- *As you do know, she is able to take astral journeys because of one of her forehead crystals, while another facilitates mental communication; a third crystal focuses on defense and offense.*

- *Her forehead crystals also created the bracelets that have enhanced powers.*

- *Once Trina came of age, she acquired crystal nails on her fingers and toes. When she asked for help from them, they gave her wrist bands and a headband that have defense and offense properties.*

- *Trina also has martial arts talents that augment her other abilities. In addition, she is able to leap and soar with ease.*

- *She also has a blue cloak that becomes a waist band when danger is present.*

- *She received some special glasses as a gift from the Creator Being that allow her to see past spells and know what is true."*

Trident shook his head as if to clear it. *"You are correct, Mother. I knew some of this, but much is new to me. My daughters are amazing!"*

Solange pressed on, *"They are, indeed. But their abilities are the product of the union of you and Terra. And YOU are the product of my union with, apparently, that mysterious Watcher who was playing the role of a royal guard. So it is important for you to acknowledge that you are a powerful magical being in your own right and, once you internalize that truth, your magic will flow more easily."*

Trident put his head in his hands and sighed, *"This is so much to absorb. Are there any spells that can help me?"*

"Possibly," responded Tamara. *"I am going to send for the Commander."*

Chapter 14
Smoothing the Way

Tamara's summons reached the Commander as he was completing his afternoon's work. He hurried to the Chapel and found a former king who was suffering under the burden of a changing reality. A worried Tamara asked him if he could be of any assistance and solace for her father.

Approaching Trident, he asked him to recline on the couch and try to relax. Chanting softly, he reached out his hands and a silver cloud descended on Trident, totally engulfing him. Tamara's bracelets began to glow, prodding her to walk to her father, placing her hands in the silver cloud and on his forehead. She felt heat and energy flow from her into her father.

As the Sisters and Trina watched in awe, Trident began to levitate and turn in the air, bringing Tamara along with him. As they drifted in the air, soft music began to play and the candles on the altar ignited. After a few minutes, Trident and Tamara returned to their original positions and the silver cloud dissipated.

"What did you do?" asked Tamara of the Commander.

"I cast a spell that brings peace and clarity. I hope it helps," he answered. Turning to Trident, he eased him to a sitting position. *"How do you feel, Sire?"* he asked.

"My head is clear and I'm no longer confused and apprehensive. Thank you, Commander," Trident replied, *"I'm grateful for your assistance."* Trident stood and started to light and extinguish candles around the Chapel. He chuckled softly to himself as he practiced his new skills. Several minutes later, he was leaping around the room, soaring higher with each effort.

"Father, please come down," implored Tamara. *"I want to ask you some questions."* Reluctantly, Trident settled on the ground next to her. *"I know you're having a good time,"* she said, *"but we need to continue exploring what you can do."*

"Such as," added Trina, *"Have any of your clothes changed?"* Trident looked at her quizzically, *"What do you mean, daughter?"* he asked. *"Clothes are clothes."* Trina sighed, *"I mean: Do any of your clothes look different than you remember them?"*

Trident thought for a while and admitted that he rarely paid attention to what he was wearing. He just put on what had been laid out for him. After another sigh, Trina asked if she could accompany him to his bedroom and look in his closet. He agreed to meet her there after lunch.

"*Meanwhile,*" continued Tamara, "*Would you try to blow up that large candle on the altar?*"

Trident turned to face the altar and extended his hands. Blue rays surged forward and vaporized the candle. "*That was easy,*" he crowed. "*I think the Commander has enabled my magic to flow!*"

"*Now, Father,*" added Tamara, "*Please create another candle to replace the one that you just destroyed.*" Trident turned back to face the altar and raised his hands once again. When blue rays reappeared, this time edged with silver, another candle was sitting in place of the vaporized one. "*Fascinating!*" he cried.

"*Well, Son,*" Solange confirmed, "*you obviously have both creative and destructive powers, which are excellent for both offense and defense.*" She suddenly threw a book at him and he raised his arms, deflecting it and sending it across the room.

"*And your defensive instincts are also working well,*" she added.

Savea nodded, approving of his handling of his newly realized abilities and suggested that they take a break and have some lunch.

*   *   *   *   *

After lunch was finished, Trina and Trident walked to

his bedroom to look in his closet. *"Is there any jacket, for example, that you wear often and really like?"* asked Trina, taking her magic glasses out of her pocket.

Trident nodded and pulled a wool jacket from the closet. *"I rather like this one,"* he said, *"but I usually grab a sweater vest with pockets so that I can carry things on my person instead of a bag."*

"Where is that vest, Father?" asked Trina, switching to mental communication and putting on the glasses.

Trident reached again into the closet and removed a grey sweater vest. *"I didn't put it on this morning for some reason, but I usually wear it every day."*

Trina peered through her glasses and gasped, *"Father, that vest has spells on it! Where did you get it?"*

"I don't know. It was just there in the closet. Once I put it on, it became my favorite."

"I'm summoning the Commander, Father," Trina insisted. *"We need to know what those spells are."*

*   *   *   *   *

It wasn't long before the Commander was knocking at the door. "How can I be of service?" he asked.

"This sweater vest of Father's has spells on it. Can you identify what they are and what they can do?" asked Trina.

"I'll try," replied the Commander, covering the vest

with a purple haze. "*If the spells are harmful or dangerous, this haze will turn black. If they are protective, the haze will turn white.*"

It wasn't long before the purple haze began to shimmer and become white before it faded away. "*Sire, I recommend that you continue to wear this vest at all times,*" said the Commander. "*Someone has gifted you with a powerful protective garment. I'm not able to tell you where it came from, but it definitely will be a positive help to you.*"

As Trina watched this interaction, her gaze moved up to her father's face. "*Father, how long have you worn glasses?*"

"*As I've grown older, my vision has declined a bit,*" he admitted. "*I sent away for some glasses to aid my reading ability. These arrived a few weeks ago.*"

"*From where?*" she asked.

"*I'm not sure. Why?*" he inquired.

"*Because they have lenses made of crystal,*" she answered. "*Do they help your vision?*"

"*They really do. I can see so much better.*"

"*How far can you see, Sire,*" asked the Commander.

"*I've been able to read signs that are quite far away,*" replied Trident .

"*Look at your vest, Father,*" directed Trina. "*Does it look any different with your glasses on?*"

"*My goodness,*" he answered. "*The vest has a glow to it. What does that mean?*"

"*I think you have received glasses that are like MY magic glasses,*" Trina suggested. "*Someone is looking out for you, Father.*"

"*That's very perceptive of you, Trina,*" praised the Commander. "I *wonder who that might be?*"

"*I think Father should ask Mother if she has any idea,*" recommended Trina. "*I think it would be a good idea to invite Mother to our next meeting.*"

Before they left the closet, Trina looked through her glasses at the rest of the clothing, but could find no other evidence of spells. Deciding that her work was done here, she recommended that they rejoin the others and return to the boat.

Chapter 15
Paying it Forward

Back on the boat, everyone had gathered once again—including Terra, who accompanied her husband at his invitation. Trident explained that there were questions which he hoped she could answer. Trina summarized what they had discovered in her father's closet and asked her mother about the spells on his vest and glasses.

Terra responded that she didn't have any definite interpretations—just thoughts about possibilities. *"What kind of possibilities, Mother,"* asked Trina.

"I agree with the Commander that Trident may be under someone's protection," she proposed. *"But I have no idea who that may be and, if I did, I would not be allowed to tell you."*

"Then it is up to us to speculate and create scenarios that seem plausible," suggested Tamara.

"And once we have several theories to test, we can follow where they lead," summarized Savea.

"Terra," Trident continued, *"What are the possibilities you are proposing?"*

"The first one that comes to mind " she began, *"is your*

father. He may have discovered that he has a son and wants to assure your well-being."

"That would be a strong possibility," agreed Solange. *"If I were he, I would do everything possible to keep Trident safe."*

"Another possibility would be Trident's twin," added Tamara. *"He may or may not be interested in your welfare, but I don't think we can eliminate him."*

"Remember that the Commander's spell revealed that those spells on Father's vest were protective, not harmful," stressed Trina. *"If it turns out to be the twin, that would definitely give us insight into his character and intentions."*

"Terra, have the Super Parents been replaced yet?" asked Tamara.

Terra nodded her head slightly.

"If they have," pondered Savea, *"They might be candidates as well. It would be smart politics to do good works to impress the Creator Being."*

The Commander added another possibility, *"If I'm not mistaken, the Creator Being also entered directly at least once by sending those magic glasses to Trina as a gift. Perhaps those spells on the vest are another gift.*

"Are there any other possible suggestions?" he asked.

"Hearing none, I recommend that we consider these

four possibilities overnight and reconvene at breakfast tomorrow."

*   *   *   *   *

When everyone had arrived at the Private Dining Room the next morning, the Commander reminded them to communicate using telepathy. He summarized the results of the previous day's discussion about who might be Trident's protector by saying, "*We have identified four possibilities so far:*

- *Trident's father, presumably the mysterious guard*

- *Trident's twin*

- *The new Super Parents*

- *The Creator Being*

"Let's consider them separately. Does anyone find Trident's father as the most likely?"

"I would like to think so," replied Solange, "*but it is dependent upon whether he even knows he has a son. And if he does, why has he not interceded before now, such as when Trident and his family were kidnapped.*"

"I think those are very important cautionary questions," agreed the Commander. "*Who else would like to propose a first choice?*"

Trident offered his choice, "*I'd like to nominate my*

twin. *Even though we haven't met, as a twin I feel a connection that he probably also feels. Perhaps he has been able to access his magic more readily than I've been able to do—at least what we know seems to confirm that.*"

"*I'd like to suggest a different approach,*" said Savea. "*Rather than vote for a positive choice, I'd like to present the least likely possibility. Solange, the Brothers, and I were produced by the then in place Super Being Parents. They had no discernible interest in Trident then, and he was of their blood line. I see no reason for a replacement set to care about him.*"

"*And that leaves the Creator Being,*" Tamara concluded. "*I believe that it is likely that my crystals are connected in some way—and certainly the glasses are—I'm not sure if direct action related to Trident is logical. I guess I see that as an open question.*"

"*So how do we proceed?*" asked Trina. "*It seems that our questions produce more questions, not answers.*"

"*I think that we practice patience,*" proposed the Commander. "*We have raised significant questions and issues. We don't know what direction to take at this time, but I believe we are aware that we must remain alert to any new developments—whether positive or hostile.*"

"*Can we agree to meet for breakfast every day to share*

any intel that has become known?" asked Tamara. "*If we hold to a regular schedule of communication, I think it will be an efficient way of monitoring events.*"

"*Won't that raise suspicions about what we might be up to?*" questioned Savea.

"*It could,*" Solange admitted, "*So I'd like to propose that we identify ourselves as a committee that has been formed to plan a festival celebrating the new year. That should provide enough cover for our meetings.*"

"*That's a great idea, Grandmother,*" said Tamara, raising her glass in a toast. "*Here's to subterfuge and a successful mission.*"

Chapter 16
Patience is Progress

Many days passed as the group gathered for breakfast 'meetings'. So far, nothing new had been reported and everyone was getting impatient.

"*Pretty soon we will need to announce the date of this festival,*" reminded Solange. "*Time is running out.*"

"*And the cover for our daily meetings will be in jeopardy,*" Tamara sighed. "*I don't understand why the Brothers haven't tried anything. The only intel I have observed is inaction.*"

"*But maybe that is actually real intel,*" stressed the Commander. "*What rationale could we imagine that would explain such inaction?*"

"*Perhaps they are working on new weapons,*" suggested Savea.

"*Or maybe some of their present plans have weaknesses that need to be addressed,*" added Trident.

"*Is it possible that your twin has escaped their custody?*" asked Trina, "*and, if so, where could he be hiding?*"

"*Do we know anything about the new Super Being*

parents? Can Terra share any information about them?" inquired Solange. "*Or would the Creator Being allow her to help us in any other way?*"

"*And what about Trident's father?*" added the Commander. "*Could Terra be allowed to give us any hints?*"

"*Do you want me to invite Mother to join us again?*" asked Tamara. "*Her name keeps coming up in our discussion.*"

There were nods of agreement around the table, so Tamara sent a mental message to Terra. After a short time, Terra boarded the boat. "*How can I be of service?*" Terra inquired.

Tamara summarized the new questions that had surfaced that morning and put special emphasis on those that referenced Terra.

"*You know I cannot be directly involved,*" Terra reminded them. "*But I think I can shed a little light for you. The new Super Being parents have a Watcher to guide them. I am not aware that they have any interest in you or this kingdom.*"

"*Then we can put them at the bottom of our list of possibilities,*" concluded the Commander. "*How about Trident's twin? Can you share anything about him?*"

"*Your hunch that he may have escaped custody has merit, but that's all I can tell you,*" Terra stated.

"*In that case,*" determined Trident, "*he goes to the top of my list, along with my father. Terra, is there anything you can tell us about my father's whereabouts?*"

"*I'm sorry, but I cannot break the code of silence that surrounds him,*" she revealed. "*However, I can encourage you to keep him on your list.*"

"*And that leaves the Creator Being,*" remarked Savea. "*Can you at least tell us if he should remain on the list?*"

"*Although his gift of magic glasses was a direct intervention, I know of no other at this time,*" she offered.

"*So our initial list of four has been reduced to two active possibilities,*" concluded Tamara. "*Thank you, Mother, for your input. I realize it was limited, but it was definitely helpful.*"

Tamara placed her hand on Terra's and asked, "*Mother, would you like to be part of our 'festival planning committee'? We were hesitant to ask, as we didn't want to put additional pressure on your Watcher responsibilities. But it occurs to me that knowing what we are up to might be a benefit to you.*"

"*It would be helpful,*" Terra agreed. "*I would be pleased to join you.*"

"*One question we did not ask you,* Mother" said Trina. "*Can you share anything about the activities and plans of the Brothers? We have discovered nothing and the inaction worries us.*"

"*I'm afraid I'm not allowed to comment at this time,*" frowned Terra, "*but it warrants continuing attention.*"

"*Then I think it's time to send out my surveillance birds again,*" proposed the Commander. "*I should have preliminary reports in a day or two.*"

"*That's a good idea,*" approved Tamara. "*And I will do my part by taking astral journeys to both Mosshire and Mesarra. Between us, we hopefully should have a current assessment of what the Brothers are up to.*"

The Sisters looked at each other and nodded. "*Meanwhile,*" Solange explained, "*Savea and I will work at enhancing our defenses with additional spells. Trident, would you assist us in this endeavor? I think it would help you explore the extent of your magic.*"

"*Of course,*" agreed Trident. "*I look forward to doing so. But I also want to work with Trina.*"

"*What am I to do?*" asked Trina. "*I'm feeling left out.*"

"*Surveillance, of course,*" answered Trident. "*You and I are the only ones with magic glasses and, when Tamara is off on her journeys, she needs to once again take your glasses with her. That leaves gaps in our monitoring of the kingdom. But with my glasses and your crystal nails, we can pick up the slack.*"

"*I do believe we have a working plan,*" approved the Commander. "*While Tamara is away, we need to keep meeting and sharing our progress. The clock is ticking.*"

Crystal Saga

8 – Making Progress

D. E. Weingand

Prologue

My name is Terra and I am the wife of Trident, the former King and now, after relinquishing the throne, a Prince of the undersea kingdom of Marinea. We have two daughters: Tamara, now the Queen of Marinea and Trina, who has recently turned seventeen. Both girls have been blessed with magic crystals. Tamara was born with one on her stomach, with more to follow as needs arose. Trina, upon reaching puberty, was gifted with crystal nails on her hands and feet. The girls keep discovering more talents and skills as time passes.

At one point, we all lived on the island of Alteria. I had met Trident walking on the beach there. We survived the great quakes which resulted in part of the island being submerged under the sea, forming the undersea kingdom of Marinea. Trident was heir to the throne and had to go to Marinea when his father passed away. The girls and I missed him so much.

Long ago, the Creator Being grew lonely and created two Super Beings to share the wonders of the universe. Those Super Beings, in turn, created mirror images of themselves and then divided them in two to limit the amount of power they possessed. We think of them as Super Children. Since that time, those original Super Being parents have been replaced because of misconduct, but the Super Children, and their subsequent mirror images, still remain: two Sisters and two Brothers. The Sisters help with the administration of Marinea; the Brothers each have a separate kingdom to rule, one in the cold North and one in the warm South of the planet.

One of the Sisters, Solange, is the mother of Trident and grandmother to our girls. The identity of Trident's father was a mystery that is beginning to unfold. Until recently, my family believed that I was without magic. When I revealed to them that I am one of the magical Watchers the Creation Being created to observe and report, but not interfere, they were astonished. But my truth has helped explain the remarkable powers that my daughters have experienced.

Another source of those powers flows through the Super Brothers. While we thought that Trident was a non-magical, we are now aware that he has significant power and are helping him learn to identify and use that power. It has become apparent that someone has been protecting him and we have formed a faux 'festival committee' that will allow us to meet regularly while investigating four possibilities that, through our analysis, has been reduced to two: Trident's mysterious father and his recently discovered twin brother.

We believe that the Brothers are working together to do harm to Marinea. We are working hard to defend our kingdom and our plan is comprehensive: The Commander of our Security Force will send his robotic birds to fly over the Brothers' kingdoms on a surveillance mission; the Sisters will focus on adding magical enhancements to our defenses; Trident and Trina have teamed up to add Trina's crystals and Trident's magical attributes to our defense strategy; and Tamara will repeat the astral journeys, facilitated by her crystals, to the Brothers' kingdoms to seek additional intel.

We must be ready to meet whatever is coming.

Chapter 1
Implementing the Plan

Tamara awoke and stretched luxuriously in bed. Suddenly she remembered that she was going to attempt her next astral journey this morning. Ringing for Mia, her attendant, she asked that breakfast be served in her bedroom.

Once her energy was restored, she hurriedly dressed in casual pants and shirt with a vest containing many pockets. One of those pockets held Trina's magic glasses that would see through any spells or magical enhancements.

Returning to her bed, she lay down and began to relax. He silver bracelets glowed, their brightness increasing as she slipped into a dream state. Feeling her spirit lift off the bed, she glanced back at her sleeping body and directed her bracelets to take her to the northern kingdom of Mosshire, ruled by the Super Brother, Sostor.

As she rapidly approached the palace in Mosshire, her speed slowed and she entered through the front door. Since she knew from past experience that she could not be seen, she explored the several floors quickly, finding nothing of importance. It seemed odd that there was so little activity in the castle and she wondered why.

Leaving the castle, she decided to use her speed to do a quick tour of the city. Few residents could be seen, which was also unusual. The city square was clearly set up to be a marketplace, but it was nearly deserted.

Tamara was puzzled. She pulled the glasses from her vest pocket and put them on. What she saw was startling. There were people everywhere, both buying and selling. What could be the purpose for hiding such normal behavior?

She returned to the palace, keeping the glasses on. Inside, staff was hustling through the halls, carrying food and drink into the ballroom. There appeared to be a gala reception in progress and Sostor was welcoming the guests. She found a good spot to stand and observe the proceedings.

Upon closer examination, the reception guests were not couples. Rather, they were primarily young men and women dressed in uniform. Puzzled, she listened carefully to what Sostor was saying. He thanked them for coming and volunteering for the new defense corps. Emphasizing how valuable their contributions were about to be, he asked them to line up at attention.

Tamara was feeling uneasy as she watched the volunteers follow his orders. Shifting her gaze to Sostor, she saw him raise his hands and send a black haze over the entire group. What had been a room full of people of normal size had become figures only a few inches high. Sostor cast a black net over the figures and had them removed from the ballroom. Calling to his aides, he ordered them to bring in the next batch of volunteers.

Deciding to follow the group of now miniature figures, Tamara slipped past the new group and went through the wall to where the first group was being loaded onto a vehicle. She hopped on the roof of the truck and rode to its final destination.

Soon they arrived at what looked like a huge warehouse made of ice. She entered the building first and found herself in the middle of multiple levels of walled cells also made of ice. As the tiny figures were shoved into cells, a grey mist surrounded them and rendered them immobile. Tamara could tell by looking in their eyes how terrified they were.

"*Is this how he is creating an army?*" she wondered. Looking around, she discovered that the cells were rapidly filling with a grey liquid, submerging the figures and creating gills on each one. "*Not just an army,*" she decided, "*but one that can live underwater. This is an attack force!*"

Rapidly touring the entire building, she found that there were many levels of cells that were already occupied by tiny figures with gills. Touching her forehead crystal that facilitated transportation, she soon found herself back in her bedroom, exhausted.

Falling into a deep sleep, she curled up in her blankets, forgetting to contact the Commander with a report of her findings.

*   *   *   *   *

The next morning, she awoke with a start, remembering that the 'festival committee' would be meeting at breakfast. She changed her clothes and hurried to the Private Dining Room.

Noting the surprised looks on everyone's faces, she quickly summarized what she had observed in Mosshire. The Commander was first to comment, "*From a tactical point of view, I would conclude that the robots we had previously encountered in Mosshire were not designed by Sostor. I say this because of the lack of evidence found by Tamara that would suggest an artificial enemy, and the overwhelming evidence of an imminent invasion by a live army—-size to be determined.*"

"*Then where do you think the robots we fought in the rescue of my family from Mosshire came from?*" asked Tamara.

"*I'm guessing that Sunan is the designer of the artificial beings, whether robotic or android in nature,*" answered the Commander.

"*That would mean that the Brothers have been working*

together from the beginning," concluded Trident, "*and any other interpretation was part of the overall masquerade.*"

"*He certainly had me fooled,*" complained Tamara. "*I trusted him when he was visiting here and shared a lot about our defenses.*"

"*We all trusted him,*" agreed Solange. "*And both Brothers even convinced me that they had been my lover on my wedding night. But we've moved on from that time of naïveté and I believe that our defenses are now secure.*"

"*So if we all believe that Sunan is the robotics mastermind, what are we to surmise about those shrunken soldiers that you saw in Mosshire?*" asked Savea.

"*Since they were altered to have gills,*" responded the Commander, "*I have to conclude that we are facing an invasion by a huge number of attackers. Reducing the size of the soldiers allows the transportation of a significant number in an efficient manner.*"

"*How can we defend ourselves against an army of unknown volume and height?*" sighed Tamara.

"*Our magic glasses will be able to see through any ruse,*" stressed Trina. "*Once we have that true intel, we can adjust our defenses to repel them.*"

"*Savea and I will create multiple spells to address several scenarios,*" promised Solange. "*At this time, I don't foresee any significant problems—given what we now know."*

"*Tamara, why do you suppose you needed the magic glasses to see that the city and the palace were not deserted?*" asked Savea.

"*I'm not sure,*" replied Tamara. "*Normal activity in the market would not have raised my suspicions. Inside the palace, however, what was taking place would definitely have been a different matter entirely. I'm guessing that the invisibility spell was designed to conceal everything and was the product of a paranoid mind.*"

"*On another matter, while I was on my journey, has the committee discovered any new intel regarding Father's alleged protector?*" asked Tamara. Seeing only negative body language, she informed them that she would undertake a second astral journey after reinforcing her energy with a substantial breakfast. This journey would be to Mesarra.

Chapter 2
A Close Look at Mesarra

After breakfast, Tamara returned to her bedroom and lay down to relax her body. Once again, her bracelets began to glow, initially with a soft light and then more strongly as she slipped into a dream state.

Her astral body moved swiftly and she soon identified the sand dunes of Mesarra. She wondered whether an invisibility spell would have also been placed here. Deciding to remain airborne, she flew over and then around the palace and its environs.

Looking down, she saw many dunes and palm trees, followed by a city and the palace itself. What she didn't see reminded her of her experience in Mosshire. There were no observable people and she reached in her pocket for the glasses. Once she donned them, she could spy many people walking around below. No danger seemed to be present, so why was there a need to produce an invisibility spell?

She flew lower to check the expressions on people's faces and found no trace of fear or anxiety. She wondered whether they could see each other—or was the spell designed to work only from above? Could it be that the Brothers had spotted the Commander's birds and created a spell to fool them? To what end? There was nothing unusual about residents walking about their city…or was there? She flew back over the people one more time and cast a spell that would enlarge her view of the faces below. That was it! The people were artificial beings, not real ones. The mystery deepened.

She sped closer to the palace and entered it through the front door. Leaving the glasses on, she walked rapidly around the palace, peering into rooms on every floor. When she reached the throne room, she saw Sunan sitting casually on the throne. He invited her to enter—but how could he see her? Other doors opened into the room and armed robots marched in, surrounding her.

Sunan stood and walked toward her. "Did you think I wouldn't figure out how you spied on us?" he demanded. But before he could cast a spell, she touched her forehead crystal and sat up in her bed, screaming.

*   *   *   *   *

The doors to Tamara's bedroom burst open and the Sisters rushed in. "What has happened?" cried Solange. "Are you all right?"

Solange sat next to Tamara on the bed and held her tightly. Shivering, Tamara sobbed and gasped, "Sunan was

8

waiting for me. Somehow he could see me. His robot soldiers surrounded me. He was about to cast a spell on me."

Solange held her hand and reminded her, *"Use telepathy, dear. We don't know who might be listening."*

Tamara nodded and tried to regain control. *"I was flying over the city toward the palace. Sunan's kingdom looked empty, like Mosshire. I put on the glasses and saw lots of people, but I was suspicious. So I cast a spell that would magnify the faces of the people directly below me and I could see that they were artificial. When I was checking out the palace, I ended in the throne room—it was a trap!"*

"How did you escape?" asked Savea.

"I touched my forehead transit crystal and it took me home," Tamara explained, still trembling.

Solange tucked the bedcovers around Tamara and urged her to rest. "I'll stay with you," Solange promised and asked Savea to call an emergency meeting of the 'festival committee.' Savea hurried from the room to summon them.

* * * * *

Savea, Tamara's family and the Commander soon knocked on her bedroom door. They pulled up chairs next to her bed and watched her with anxious faces. Solange was seated on the bed, her arm around Tamara's shoulders. Terra sat on the other side of Tamara, holding her hand. Solange thanked them for coming so promptly and briefly summarized what Tamara had shared with her earlier.

Tamara was still trembling, but straightened up and began to speak. "*I am very afraid for our kingdom,*" she began. "*It is clear to me that the Brothers have been working together all along and doing everything in their power to confuse and mislead us. I have no way of knowing their timetable for an attack, but I am certain that it will not be long until we feel the first stage. Commander, have your birds added any intel to what I have observed?*"

"*My birds have discovered nothing out of the ordinary. However, to them, the ordinary can be interpreted as recognizing nothing. So when an invisibility spell is at work, they would not notice a problem. I have to do some research on spells that can be more selective and discerning. I will let you know what I find,*" he replied. "*Meanwhile, Sisters, what have you been up to with improving our defenses?*"

"*After Tamara reported her findings in Mosshire,*" responded Savea, "*we worked on ways to obstruct or eliminate any incoming army, regardless of size. The last time an attack force approached, it was confined to a tunnel. Now, since the soldiers have gills, they would have much more freedom to maneuver. It definitely complicates matters.*"

"*So we have decided to fortify all possible entries to the kingdom,*" added Solange. "*We have designed and built a larger dome to cover the kingdom. The space between the domes is filled with spells equipped with artificial intelligence (AI) that automatically repositions the spells to address dangerous situations. There is no way for invaders to anticipate where these spells might be located—or relocated.*"

"*Are the invaders eliminated or taken prisoner,*" asked Tamara.

"*Hopefully, the latter,*" explained Savea. "*If everything works correctly, the invaders would be rendered unconscious and transported to a holding facility located between the domes. Based on Tamara's intel, we recognize that the invasion force is composed of volunteer citizen soldiers who did not understand what they were being required to do. To conserve space, there are spells in place to reduce them in size again if necessary.*"

"*I'm impressed,*" congratulated the Commander. "*You have been very clever in your approach to keeping the kingdom safe. Have you implemented all of your ideas or is there more to do?*"

"*We have completed what we set out to do,*" responded Solange. "*However, there may be adjustments to make once the attack is underway.*"

Trident and Trina looked at each other and smiled at the Sisters. "*We applaud your efforts as well,*" said Trident. "*Since our mission is focused more on hand-to-hand combat, we have been practicing our skills and feel that we have become more proficient. If you all approve, we would like to take point on identifying my protector. We believe that he may be important in the conflict to come.*"

Terra kissed Tamara's cheek and stood. "*I must leave to make a report,*" she explained. "*I will return as soon as possible.*"

Tamara smiled at her mother and, thanking everyone for their contributions, lay back on her bed. Within seconds, her eyes had closed and she had entered a dream state. Her bracelets began to glow…

Chapter 3
The Unexpected Journey

Tamara felt herself flying, but she hadn't given her bracelets a destination. Puzzled, she wondered where they were taking her. She flew higher and higher until she began to recognize where she was headed: the Crystal Castle. Now she was truly confused. Why would her bracelets be taking her here?

As she arrived at the Castle, she walked inside and climbed the stairs to the top level. When she had been here before, this was where the orb of power was located and the Super Being parents had resided. So far, she had not seen anyone.

Putting on her magic glasses, she looked around more carefully. Unlike her journey to the kingdoms ruled by the Brothers, there was no difference in what she saw with or without the glasses. That was comforting, she thought as she continued to explore.

Hearing voices ahead, she moved through a wall and found what she assumed were the new Super Beings and two older Beings seated around a table that was laden with food.

The older woman stood and walked toward her, saying "Welcome, Tamara. It is lovely to meet you."

"You can see me?" asked Tamara. "How is that possible?"

"Yes, we can both see and hear you," replied the woman. "My name is Elsa and I am a Watcher. Let me introduce you to the others: On my right is Rogere, also a Watcher; next to him are Adele and Jeremy, the current Super Beings. We were just sharing a meal. Would you like to join us? Here in the Castle, you are able to eat, even in astral form."

Tamara nodded and another chair appeared at the table. As she sat down, a plate piled with food materialized before her. Picking up a fork, she tasted the food and found it to be delicious.

"We were surprised when you arrived," said Elsa. "Terra did not tell us you were coming."

"She didn't know," replied Tamara. "I didn't know. My bracelets brought me here without being directed by me. How is it that you can see and hear me? On my previous journeys, I was invisible and silent."

"This Castle contains a huge crystal of power that can do marvelous things," explained Elsa. "I suspect that the Creator Being brought you here via your bracelets. There must be a purpose in such an action. It might be related to our mission here.

"Rogere and I are Watchers, but also Guardians of the two Super Beings," she continued. Watcher Terra had reported that previous Super Being couples failed to behave appropriately and were eliminated. She recommended that Guardians be appointed to act as parents and role models so that subsequent pairs might learn how to act positively toward each other and related beings. I believe that our efforts are bearing fruit. Adele and Jeremy are kind and caring beings, although they have yet to meet the offspring of prior couples. Now, why do you think you are here?"

Tamara explained that she had not directed her bracelets to come to the castle. However, she and her family and friends had been working on several problems. One concerned the Super Brothers and their apparently hostile intentions toward her kingdom. Another was the identity of her father's father, which was a mystery. A third was to discover who might be serving as a protector of her father through the creation of spells discovered on his clothing and belongings.

"Ah," said Elsa. "Since it seems that your bracelets wish to help you solve these problems, let's consider them. Adele and Jeremy have not met your family, so I think we can rule them out. That would leave Rogere and me. Our mission has been to be parents and role models for Adele and Jeremy, so we have not had any contact with the Brothers. Rogere, have you been involved with the other two problems that Tamara has described? I know that I have not."

Rogere shifted uneasily in his chair and finally admitted that he had, but was not at liberty to discuss it.

"Why not?" asked Elsa. "For heaven's sake, this girl certainly has a right to the solutions to those two questions."

"The Creator Being has forbidden it," responded Rogere sadly.

Tamara walked around the table to where Rogere was sitting and asked, "May I place my hands on your head?"

"For what purpose?" he responded.

"You are sad and agitated. I wish to soothe you," she replied.

He agreed and she gently placed her hands on his brow. Chanting softly, she placed him in a relaxed state and mentally probed his thoughts.

"I'd really like her to know that I am her Grandfather," he thought, *"but I have been told not to speak of it. She's such a lovely girl, so much like her Grandmother."*

Tamara smiled gently, wishing she could hug him and admit that she knew the truth. However, she felt obligated to respect his wishes and his privacy.

Before she said goodbye to this congenial group, she

decided to ask Elsa more about their mission. "How long have you been Guardians to the Super Beings?"

"Since they were created," responded Elsa. "Terra pointed out how improvements could be made if Guardians would assume a parental role. That must be a couple of generations by now."

"That's not possible," challenged Tamara. "I was here in the Castle when the last pair of Super Beings were misbehaving."

"Remember that time operates differently here in the castle," said Elsa. "Before I was appointed Guardian, I had already lived several generations as a Watcher on Alteria."

"So that's when you and Terra became friends?" asked Tamara.

"Yes," acknowledged Elsa. "I was with her when you were born. That crystal on your stomach must have been quite a shock to your parents."

"So much so that we kept it a secret until I reached puberty and its effects became visible," replied Tamara.

"What about Rogere?" she added. "What did he do before becoming a Guardian?"

"He had a special mission as a Watcher in service to the kings of Marinea. He doesn't talk about it, though," Elsa replied.

"And I am still not allowed to do so," reminded Rogere. "Let's drop the subject."

Tamara nodded and thanked them for their hospitality. She touched her transit crystal and found herself back in her bed.

Chapter 4
Another Piece of the Puzzle

Tamara sat up in bed, surprised to find the entire team still around her. *"You're here!"* she exclaimed.

"You've only been gone a few minutes," commented Savea. *"Where did you go this time?"*

"It seems that the Creator Being allowed me to solve one of our problems," Tamara explained. *"My bracelets took me to the Crystal Castle. I met the new Super Beings and their two Guardians. Mother, the female Guardian is your old friend, Elsa. She told me she was present when I was born!"*

"Really!" cried Terra. *"I'm so pleased that you could meet her. We've lost touch over the years."*

"And there's more," added Tamara. *"These Guardians are implementing YOUR recommendations about parenting. From what I've observed, this new set of Super Beings is vastly different from the ones I had to interact with."*

"That's really wonderful to hear," responded Terra. *"I know that Elsa has a good heart. But what about her male partner? What did you think of him?"*

Smiling at her mother, Tamara rose and embraced her

grandmother. "*I have important news for you. His name is Rogere. While he had indicated that he was forbidden by the Creator Being to discuss his past, he gave me permission to place my hands on his head and I was able to access his thoughts.*

"*I am convinced that he was the guard who was in the room with you when you were married to the mysterious king's son. He is a Watcher and his mission was to observe the two kings. I believe that he was your lover during that time, but I don't know if he ever realized that you were pregnant. Since that is uncertain, I find it hard to point to him as father's protector.*"

Solange clasped Tamara's hand and asked, "*Are you certain? Have we identified Trident's father at last?*"

"*I'm confident that he is,*" replied Tamara, "*but there are still questions to investigate, such as whether he knows anything about Father and why the Creator Being has mandated his silence.*"

"*It seems like every time we get closer to an answer, more questions arise,*" complained Trident. "*However, I have to admit that I am much happier about Rogere as my father than either of the Brothers.*"

"*I agree with you, Son,*" Solange added, "*From what Tamara relates, Rogere seems like a worthy parent for you.*

Now, I must insist that we allow Tamara to rest and recoup her energy. Shall we all meet for dinner and continue this conversation?"

Nodding agreement, the group dispersed and Tamara snuggled into her bedcovers. No one noticed that her bracelets were glowing again.

*   *   *   *   *

As Tamara reentered a dream state, she felt herself airborne once more. Confused that she would be traveling once more without taking time for resting, she looked around and noticed that the terrain beneath her was turning white. *"There must be some urgency,"* she thought. *"I wonder what that could be."*

In a few minutes, she began to recognize the landscape of Mosshire. Now she was increasingly puzzled because her last encounter with the Brothers was in Mesarra. Slowing down, she dropped to the ground at the front entrance to the palace.

Walking inside, she heard voices coming from the kitchen at the rear of the palace. "Do we know when the king will return?" asked one voice. "I haven't heard anything," said another voice. "So we are preparing food just for the staff and the prisoner?" inquired the first voice. "That's right," said the second voice. "How long has the prisoner been in our dungeon?" asked a third voice. "Since he became of age, years ago. The rumor is that he's a very talented magical and the Brothers are trying to control him," added a fourth voice.

Startled by this new information, Tamara headed toward the stairway leading to the dungeon. She was relieved to discover that Sostor was not in residence and decided to locate this mysterious prisoner.

Moving quickly down the stairway, she peered into every cell as she passed through the dungeon. Finally, as the end of the hall, she reached a cell that looked more like a well-appointed bedroom than a cell. There was a man sitting at a desk and she gasped in recognition. He looked just like her father, although his hair hadn't been cut in some time.

The man turned and greeted her. "Hello," he said. "It's nice to have a visitor. Who are you?"

"My name is Tamara," she answered. "I'm surprised that you can see me."

"I can hear you, as well," he offered. "Since you are silent in your movement, may I assume that you are on an astral journey?"

"What do you know about astral journeys?" she inquired.

"Quite a bit, actually," he admitted. "I would have lost my mind long ago if I hadn't learned how to take them and leave the confines of this cell. Can you also communicate telepathically?"

"*I can,*" she told him mentally. "*Can you hear me when I do so?*"

"*Loud and clear!!!*" he cried, also mentally.

"*Then I think we should talk only mentally from now on,*" she recommended. "*There are probably listening devices around.*"

"*There were,*" he replied, "*but I disabled them.*"

"*Hasn't Sostor noticed that they aren't working?*" she asked.

"*He did, at first. But as soon as he reactivated them, I would disable them again. Finally, he grew tired of doing so and left me alone,*" he bragged.

"*I'm impressed,*" she told him. "*However, I wouldn't assume anything if I were you. He's a very clever and powerful sorcerer.*"

"*I know,*" he agreed, "*but then, so am I. I may be self-taught, but my skills are many. The Brothers keep trying to control me, but they haven't been able to—which is why my physical body is down here.*"

"*When did they capture you and put you in this dungeon?*" she asked.

"*When I came of age, I discovered that I had magic.*"

The Brothers came soon after. They seemed to know," he concluded.

"And before that? Where did you live?" Tamara probed.

"My earliest memories are that of a young child," he responded. *"I lived with a couple that I thought were my parents. They were not wealthy, but we were rich with love. It was a happy childhood."*

"When did you find out that they were not your parents?" she asked.

"When I came of age, they told me the whole story," he responded. *"Apparently, an unknown man came to their home with me wrapped in a blanket. He paid them to care for me. Payments kept appearing throughout my time there."*

"Do you know that you are an identical twin?" Tamara asked.

"I do," he admitted. *"I was connecting with him by accident and then I took astral journeys to visit him. I never understood why he could not see or hear me."*

"Now it's my turn for full disclosure," promised Tamara. *"I am the Queen of the undersea kingdom of Marinea. My father was once the king and I became Queen when he and my mother and sister were kidnapped by Sostor. Once we rescued my family, he reevaluated his life choices and abdicated in my favor. He is your twin.*

"*He could not hear or see you because, all his life, he had believed that he was a non-magical,*" Tamara related. "*We all lived on the island of Alteria together until great quakes occurred and part of the island broke off and sank into the sea. The short version of this story is that the two female Super Beings lived in the sea and helped survivors live under the sea by giving them gills. Someday, we'll sit down together and I'll fill in the blanks.*"

"*When we talk, you may be surprised at how much cosmology I know,*" he commented. "*Part of the Brothers' attempt to control me included a detailed education—although undoubtedly from their point of view.*"

"*When you take your next astral journey,*" she suggested, "*please try to contact my father again. He has learned that he has magic that runs through him from HIS parents: his mother, Solange, one of the Super Sisters, and a newly-discovered father who is also magical.*"

Tamara walked through the cell bars and hugged her uncle. "*Since I am family, would you tell me your name?*" she asked.

"*My foster parents named me Trillium,*" he shared. "*I am delighted to discover that I have a family. Quick, hide yourself. I hear someone coming.*"

Tamara crossed to an empty cell and watched a kitchen

staffer bring a meal to Trillium. The staffer commented that the king had suddenly returned and might want to talk to Trillium.

Tamara reached her hand toward her transit crystal and let Trillium know that she must leave. Promising that she would return soon, she touched her crystal and awoke on her bed.

Chapter 5
Reunion

Tamara called for Mia and asked for help dressing for dinner. She needed to meet with the committee as soon as possible.

*   *   *   *   *

Entering the Private Dining Room, she hurried over to the table where her committee was already seated. *"Did you have a good rest?"* asked Solange.

"I had no rest at all," sighed Tamara. *"As soon as you all left my room, I was taken on another astral journey. I have to admit that I'm really tired!"*

Terra took her daughter's hand and Tamara felt soothing energy flow into her. *"Thank you, Mother,"* she said. *"That helped a lot."*

"Now tell us where you went and what you learned," ordered the Commander.

"My bracelets took me to Mosshire," Tamara related. *"When I entered the palace, I heard voices in the kitchen and I went to listen."*

Tamara summarized what she had heard in the kitchen

and, subsequently, in the dungeon. Her description of the conversation with Trident's twin had everyone mesmerized. Clearly, no one had expected such important intel.

The Commander approved of her decision to leave the dungeon as soon as she became aware that Sostor had returned. *"Since you had discovered on your previous trip that the Brothers had developed a way to hear and see you, it was very prudent that you returned home. Do you have any idea what they found to counteract your invisibility?"*

"I have no idea," she replied. *"I escaped Mesarra as soon as I found out. Perhaps it was a spell. I don't know.*

"But after conversing with Trillium, I don't believe the Brothers have figured out that he can also take astral journeys," she decided. *"By the way, Father, I think you can expect him to contact you soon. Please be open to him when he does. He's very excited about meeting you."*

"Do you think he has been Trident's protector?" asked Solange.

"I don't know," Tamara replied. *"We had to discontinue our conversation before I had a chance to investigate further. However, I wouldn't rule it out. He's a very skilled magical being."*

"How will I know that he is trying to contact me?" asked Trident.

"*Think back, Father,*" advised Tamara. "*Until you acknowledged your magic, you couldn't see or hear me mentally. What changed?*"

"*Of course, you are correct.*" Trident admitted. "*Once I believed that I had magic, many other abilities fell into place.*"

"*Father, please make sure that the chair next to you remains empty,*" smiled Tamara. "*Trillium has just joined us. Can you see him?*"

Trident looked at the previously empty chair and gasped, "*I can! It's like looking into a mirror.*"

The astral image of Trillium smiled at Trident and said, "*It's nice to finally meet you, Brother. We have a lot to catch up on.*" The others at the table, having magic of their own and able to see and hear the twins, also smiled as the twins began to share memories.

Tamara leaned back in her chair, her hand brushing the pocket holding the magic glasses. On impulse, she pulled them out and put them on. Horrified, she yelled, "*Stop!*" Reaching out her hands, she directed a blue ray at the image of Trillium, shattering it into tiny fragments.

"*Why did you do that?*" cried Trident, horrified.

Shaking, she answered, "*Because it wasn't Trillium. It was Sostor in disguise! When I left Trillium in Mosshire, Sostor was about to visit him. Sostor must have figured out that*

Trillium could travel astrally and decided to take advantage of the opportunity to gather intel about us."

"*We must remember how powerful a sorcerer Soster is,*" admonished Tamara. "*He has obviously learned that Trillium can travel on the astral plane, and somehow he has substituted himself in the guise of Trillium. We need to remain vigilant and use the glasses whenever possible.*"

"*Since our connection with the astral plane has been compromised,*" advised Savea, "*it is imperative that we rescue Trillium from that dungeon. How shall we go about doing that?*"

"*What is the status of that tunnel that we used to rescue Father?*" asked Tamara.

Savea answered, "*It is not usable right now, but I can fix that by tomorrow.* "

"*That's a good start,*" approved Tamara, "*but I don't think we should do the same plan that we did before. How can we make substantive changes that are not easily detected?*"

"*I think we need a diversion,*" proposed the Commander. "*When Savea has made the tunnel operational again, I will cast the multiplier spell on my birds and attack the palace. That should attract their attention.*"

"*And while all this is going on,*" added Solange, "*I will bring a storm in off the sea that will both confuse and hamper any hostile activities that may be underway."*

"*I definitely cannot take an astral journey this time, so I will accompany the attack force in real time,*" decided Tamara.

"*With the rest of your family at your side,*" added Trident. "*This is definitely a family affair.*"

Chapter 6
The Family Rescue

The next day, all assault strategies were in place and Tamara entered the tunnel, followed by her family and the assault force. As they progressed through the tunnel, she turned to Savea and began, *"Last time, you caused the tunnel to do a U-turn and exit back at Mosshire. Are you going to do that again? If you haven't decided, may I suggest that you create a camouflaged exit door just before you turn the tunnel. That way, we could safely return to Marinea after rescuing Trillium and still confuse any pursuers by having them wind up back where they started."*

"That's an interesting twist," approved Savea. "I will definitely work that into my design."

Nearing Mosshire, Savea halted and cast several spells that resulted in a tunnel extension to Mosshire that was shaped like the letter C. However, just before the beginning of the extension, the existing tunnel appeared to end with a magical door in place. At the point where the old and new tunnels connected, one-half of the extension was covered with an invisibility spell that would be removed after the rescue was completed. The overall effect was a tunnel extension that appeared to head directly to Mosshire.

"That looks perfect!" Tamara crowed. As she entered the tunnel extension, she stopped and cast an invisibility spell backwards to cover the assault force and her family. Proceeding quickly, yet carefully, they emerged from the extension and ran across the storm-tossed land to the entrance of the palace. Overhead, they heard the screeching of the Commander's robot birds as they dive-bombed the palace.

Slipping into the palace entryway, she unlocked the door and led everyone into the hallway. Racing toward the stairway leading to the dungeon, she hurried down the stairs and ran to Trillium's cell. Putting on the magic glasses to confirm that Trillium was real, she opened his cell door and pulled him into the hall. "We've come for you. Please follow me quickly," she urged.

Trident hugged his twin and stepped into the cell to create the illusion of a sleeping Trillium on the bed. Following the rear of the assault force, he joined them in heading toward the tunnel entrance. The wind howled and rain lashed the rescue party as they reached the tunnel,

Tamara looked back at the palace and thought, *"This was too easy. There's something we're not seeing."*

Just then, the robotic birds that had been dive bombing

the palace turned and headed straight for them. *"Sostor must be interfering with their programming!"* she cried. *"Get under water and into the tunnel as quickly as you can!"* Spinning around, she erected a wall to disrupt the robotic attack. As the birds crashed into the wall, she watched with dismay as Soster's miniature army erupted from the palace, gaining height and stature as they headed toward the beach. Raising her arms, she hurled a green fog toward them, slowing them down dramatically. As soon as the assault force had completely entered the tunnel extension, she followed them and sealed the entrance behind her.

When she arrived at the midpoint of the tunnel extension, she asked Trina to open the entrance she had just sealed and unlock the magic door to the original tunnel. Scrambling behind the magic door, Tamara released the invisibility spell on the second half of the tunnel extension and repositioned it over the magic door as Trina locked it again. Now when Sostor's army came upon the magic door, they would be unable to see it and, instead, would follow the now visible tunnel extension back toward shore.

"That was close," she thought. Turning to Savea, she asked her to reseal the tunnel as she had before and directed Trina to put up periodic barriers within the tunnel to slow down any pursuers.

Racing to catch up with her family and the assault force, she finally decided to walk beside her mother, following her father and his twin. Linking arms, she teased, *"Well, you will have a lot to report now, Mother."*

"Indeed I will," agreed Terra. *"Thankfully, you were able to outwit Sostor. More than one outcome was possible. When we arrive in Marinea, I will need to leave you for a short time to make that report."*

"I understand," replied Tamara. *"Please hurry back as I will be convening the committee to plan future strategies. But first, I want to have a conversation with Father and Trillium."*

"That should be very interesting," approved Terra. *"I would like to sit in on that meeting before I make my report."*

"Understood," Tamara replied, *"but please regard what you hear as classified intel and only include in your report what you deem absolutely necessary."*

"Of course," agreed Terra. *"I'm so happy to see that we have reached our kingdom. It's been a long and stressful day."*

*   *   *   *   *

Tamara asked her father and uncle to accompany her to the Commander's office. When they arrived, she briefed the Commander on what had taken place during the Mosshire mission and informed him that his birds had been compromised.

"*I'm not surprised that Sostor was able to alter the birds' programming. He is a very talented and powerful sorcerer. I will have to redesign the birds completely before sending them out again,*" he decided. "*Do you think the tunnel has been breached?*" he asked.

"*I don't know,*" responded Tamara. "*Savea and Trina erected defensive barriers, but we didn't wait around to see if they held.*"

"*While you were gone, I had cameras installed along the full length of the tunnel,*" the Commander related. "*Those screens on the far wall will tell us.*"

Tamara viewed the screens with trepidation, but she saw nothing unusual in the tunnel. With relief, she congratulated the Commander on his ingenuity.

Reaching into her pocket, she once again put on her magic glasses. Gesturing toward nearby chairs, she invited everyone to sit down. "*This conversation is highly classified and nothing should leave this room,*" she ordered. "*Trillium, we only communicate mentally in this kingdom until all danger has passed. Father, have you and your brother shared any information on the walk back from Mosshire?*"

While Trident responded to her question, she focused her glasses on Trillium. She noticed that his image was slightly out of focus, which worried her. The glasses had always been accurate in discovering false images and intel; this was a new and disturbing feature. Perhaps this was why their departure from Mosshire had been so uneventful.

She locked eyes with the Commander and sent him a personal message describing her concern. His lips began to move silently and a purple haze filled the room. Everyone froze in place as a second haze, this time white in color, covered everything in the room—including the vid screens. Although she could not move physically, she looked at the screens in horror! The tunnel had been infiltrated by the tiny army and were almost to Marinea!

As the two hazes dissipated and movement returned, Trillium shivered and what looked like an exoskeleton slid to the floor. Before her stood Sostor, with an evil smile on his face.

Chapter 7
Unmasking the Truth

"How??" stammered Tamara.

"You thought you were so smart, didn't you?" crowed Sostor.

"Where is my brother?" demanded Trident.

"Beyond your reach, and he shall remain there," boasted Sostor. "Don't bother using telepathy. I can hear and see you no matter what you try. Sunan and I have powers that you have never even dreamed of!"

So engaged in bragging about his powers, Sostor didn't notice Terra, who was sitting near the door. She shimmered briefly and disappeared.

Solange tried to keep Sostor's attention away from the chair where Terra had been sitting and asked, "What are you trying to prove, Sostor? Are you so insecure that you need to expand your influence beyond what your parents gave you?"

"Be careful of trying to provoke me," Sostor snarled. My brother and I are stronger than you can imagine. Your powers are weak compared to ours!"

"How do you know?" retorted Solange. "None of our

powers have been tested or measured."

"Sunan and I have been monitoring you for generations. We have developed the means to siphon off your powers for our own use," he claimed. "And we plan to use Tamara as our personal power supply!"

Tamara blanched and her bracelets began to glow. "Is that so?" she said calmly. "How do you expect to do that?"

"Like this…" he said, raising his arms and expelling a black cloud.

Tamara's arms also rose, blocking the cloud and sending it back toward Sostor. Her bracelets wove the cloud into ropes and bound Sostor so that he couldn't move. He squealed and began to chant as he struggled to get free. Solange wrapped him in an additional layer of restraint, covering his mouth, and asked, *"Commander, don't you have an isolation cell that we could park Sostor in?"*

The Commander smiled and called his aide to assist him in the transport. Looking over his shoulder, he said, *"Tamara, better take care of that tiny army in the tunnel."*

"Right," agreed Tamara. *"I'll get right on it!"*
After thinking for a minute, she asked Savea and Trina to gather the Security Force and head toward the tunnel.

"The nerve of that Sostor!" exclaimed Solange after they had left. *"When Terra returns, perhaps she will have some*

advice as to how we should handle him permanently."

"*Maybe,*" replied Tamara, "*but let's not forget that there is another Super Brother that we have yet to deal with.*"

"*And I have a brother that was lost, then found, now lost again,*" reminded Trident.

"*Our problems seem to multiply, Father,*" she admitted. "*But we will tackle them, one by one.*"

*　　　*　　　*　　　*　　　*

Savea and Trina reached the airlock next to the Practice Field and stepped inside. The Security Force lined up behind them. It took several minutes for everyone to gather in the tunnel. Savea took charge of the group and issued instructions. Noting that the vid screens had displayed the army as being composed of tiny figures, she explained that their size might have changed since that viewing.

Moving cautiously ahead, they came upon a host of tiny figures lying prone on the ground. She picked up one of the figures and checked for signs of life. Chanting softly, she sent a cloud of white haze down the tunnel. Her spell was designed to identify life signs. Sadly, she turned to the Security Force and reported that no life had been detected.

Trina asked her what had happened and Savea surmised that when Sostor had been put in an isolation cell, he had been cut off from any spells that he had in place. Her guess was that the gills on the tiny army had failed and they had drowned.

Casting another spell, a dark blue haze in color that would dissolve the bodies as they proceeded, Savea led the group through the tunnel and reactivated and reinforced all the barriers along the way. No opposition was encountered.

When they reached the end of the tunnel where it had connected with the tunnel extension, she erected additional barriers and sealed off that juncture. Afterwards, they reversed course and returned to Marinea.

*   *   *   *   *

When Savea, Trina and the Security Force reemerged on the Practice Field, they were greeted by Tamara and her mother, Terra. "Mother, I'm so happy you're back!" cried Trina, throwing her arms around Terra. Terra returned the hug and walked with both her daughters into the palace while Savea left to report events to the Commander.

Savea knocked on the Commander's office door. When bidden to enter, she did so and settled herself into a chair. The Commander sat across from her and invited her to report. After explaining what had happened to the tiny army, he leaned back and said, "*I never anticipated that. I didn't realize how closely connected spells are to the spell caster. That is very useful information.*"

There was a series of raps at the door and Tamara,

Trident and Terra entered, with Trina and Solange close behind. *"We thought you might have come here, Savea,"* explained Tamara. *"We need to talk about how these recent events might influence our future planning."*

Terra interrupted, *"And I need to brief you on my meeting with the Creator Being."*

Tamara nodded to Terra and indicated that she should proceed. Terra stood and walked over to the vid screens. She pointed to the image of the tiny army lying prone on the tunnel floor. *"This was unanticipated. It will revolutionize the way we detain or incarcerate magical felons in the future. But that is a discussion for another day. Our mission now is to decide how to proceed with Sunan. Sostor has been taken off the game board, at least for the present."*

"What will become of his kingdom?" asked Tamara. *"Who will rule it?"*

"An interim ruler has been appointed," responded Terra. *"You will find this interesting. He has been a Guardian of the present Super Beings and is now being reassigned temporarily to Mosshire."*

Solange grew pale and probed, *"Is this the Guard that was present on my wedding night?"*

"The very same," answered Terra. *"We will need a longer conversation about this, but know that the idea came*

from the Creator Being, not me."

"*So my true father will be on our plane of existence,*" concluded Trident. "*What is the Creator Being's endgame?*"

"*I don't know,*" admitted Terra. "*I am just following orders.*"

"*We need to digest this new development,*" said Tamara. "*Let's meet for breakfast tomorrow morning to continue our conversation.*"

Chapter 8
A New Player on the Board

Sitting around the breakfast table, the "Festival Committee" members were strangely quiet. "*Mother*," Tamara finally asked, "*Does he know he is the father of the twins?*"

"*I was not given that information*," sighed Terra, "*so I think we must approach him with caution.*"

"*I agree,*" affirmed Tamara. "*Perhaps another astral journey is indicated. Do you think this new Watcher would be willing to share any information?*"

"*Possibly,*" Terra replied. "*However, as personally interesting as that journey might be, I think Mesarra could be of more importance.*"

Savea interrupted, "*Yes! We need to learn about his plans of attack. I realize that it would be risky for you, Tamara, since he apparently can know when you are present. Commander, are there any spells that could shield Tamara from him?*"

"*I don't know of any,*" he admitted. "*But, Tamara, couldn't you ask your bracelets for added cover?*"

"*Of course!*" she explained. "*Why didn't I think of*

that. Savea, would you come with me? I would feel so much more comfortable if I had your backup."

"*Certainly,*" agreed Savea. "*When shall we leave?*"

"*Since this is an urgent mission, I suggest that we depart immediately after we finish breakfast,*" Tamara replied.

*   *   *   *   *

Within the hour, Tamara and Savea were lying next to each other on Tamara's bed. As Tamara relaxed into a dream state, Savea could feel the tension leave her own body and she held Tamara's hand.

Within her dream state, Tamara asked her bracelets to shield her from Sunan during the journey. She didn't notice when her bracelets were covered with a silver glaze. A silver glaze also appeared on Savea's wrists.

Hand-in-hand, the astral bodies of the two women flew through the air and they soon saw sand dunes ahead. Reaching the palace, they dropped to the ground and entered through the wall next to the main entrance. Tamara put on her glasses and observed that, once again, the potted plants along the corridor were actually armed robot guards.

Walking down the hallway, they came to an open door and peered inside. Sitting in comfortable chairs in front of a table covered with documents and charts, Sunan and an aide were discussing strategies for the upcoming attack on Marinea.

Tamara reached out her hands toward a window and opened it, inviting a strong breeze to enter and blow everything off the table. Startled, Sunan and his aide leaped up and began to gather the papers from the floor. As they retrieved the papers that had blown away and returned them to the table top, the aide knocked over a candle that had remained on the table, causing the papers to catch fire. Within minutes, only ashes remained.

Sunan began to scream insults at his aide, who ran fearfully from the room. *"I think we may have delayed the attack,"* commented Tamara. *"Let's see what he does next."*

Striking the table with his hand, Sunan stormed out of the room and headed toward a nearby staircase. Climbing to the next floor, he moved quickly down the hall and stopped at a closed door. Waving his hand, he unlocked the door and stepped inside.

Tamara and Savea had followed him up the stairs and entered the room through the wall. Pausing inside the room, they were surprised to see a cell with walls that pulsated with magical power. Inside sat a prisoner who looked just like Trident. Adjusting her glasses, Tamara noted that the image of the prisoner didn't change, and said to Savea, *"That must actually be Trident's twin. The glasses don't indicate any active spells other than the cell walls.*"

Savea nodded in agreement and suggested, "*Let's just listen and observe.*"

Sunan pulled a chair up to the cell and sat down. "Well, Trillium, have you come to your senses yet?" he asked. "If you agree to my plan, I can release you."

Trillium turned away and stayed silent. Sunan stood and began pacing the floor. "Don't be stupid," he sneered. "Do you really want to spend your life in this cell? Remember that I was the only one to be kind to you. I discovered you; I made it possible for you to attend the magic academy; I'm the only friend you have ever had!!!"

"*Well, now we know who his benefactor was,*" commented Savea.

"I wonder if we can communicate with him without Sunan hearing?" asked Tamara. "Shall I try?"

Savea nodded.

As Tamara began to speak mentally, the silver on her bracelets began to pulsate. "*Trillium, my name is Tamara. I am queen of Marinea and I am here on the astral plane. With me is my Great Aunt Savea, who is a Super Being. If you can hear me, raise your right arm.*"

Trillium stood and stretched his right arm above his head. "*Do you know that you are a twin?*" asked Tamara. "*If you do, sit down again.*" Trillium sat. "*Do not attempt to speak to me mentally while Sunan is in the room. He is capable of hearing you. Just follow my instructions,*" continued Tamara.

"*If you know who your twin is, look at the floor,*" added Tamara. Trillium didn't move.

"*Your twin is my father, Trident, the former king of Marinea. We only learned of your existence very recently because you were taken from your mother at birth. We have been searching for you,*" Tamara related. "*I will stay here until Sunan leaves the room and then we can have a conversation.*"

Meanwhile, Sunan continued to harangue Trillium, shouting and waving his arms. Recognizing that Trillium was continuing to ignore him, he left the room, slamming the door behind him.

Savea went toward the door and offered to check that Sunan had actually left. In a moment, she returned and nodded.

"*He's gone, Trillium,*" assured Tamara. "*You may speak mentally now.*" She was surprised when some of the silver on her left wrist slipped under the cell wall closest to her and encircled Trillium's wrists.

"*What just happened?*" asked Trillium mentally.

"*I believe my magic bracelets decided to make sure that our conversation would be private,*" she responded. "*But I don't know how they managed to reach you inside that warded cell.*"

"*I do,*" he answered. "*When Sunan was placing the wards on the cell, I was quietly making the floor drop just a bit. There is a space there that is open and I've made use of it.*"

"*How?*" asked Savea.

"*I can reduce myself in size and crawl through,*" Trillium explained. "*I've been spying on Sunan for a long time.*"

"*Really!*" exclaimed Savea. "*Your magical skills are truly impressive. What can you tell us about Sunan's plans for invasion?*"

"*The invasion will come later,*" he explained. "*His first intention is to exchange me for your father, Tamara. He wants me to agree to facilitate the invasion, while he holds your father hostage. So far, I have been able to avoid becoming complicit in this plan.*"

"*So far?*" asked Tamara. "*What leverage does he hold over you?*"

"*Continued captivity in this cell, for one example. Need I even mention that he has extensive experience in methods of torture?*" he added.

"*What are Sunan's weaknesses?*" asked Savea.

"*He fears that something may happen to his brother,*" replied Trillium. "*Should that happen, since they are identical twins that were once one being, he would also die."*

"*Does he know that we have captured Sostor and are holding him in a magically enhanced isolation cell?*" asked Tamara.

"*Because they have the closeness of twins, he probably suspects,*" replied Trillium. "*But the isolation cell may cause him to be uncertain.*"

"*You are a twin, but you were not aware of my father,*" prodded Tamara.

"*I had glimpses of his thoughts and intentions, but I did not know what those feelings meant,*" explained Trillium. "*Now that I am aware that we are twins, I can better interpret those glimpses.*"

"*What now, Trillium?*" asked Savea. "*Do you want to come with us or remain here?*"

Trillium smiled, and his body shrunk before their eyes. As he crawled out of the cell, he asked Tamara to put him in her pocket. "*But I'm on the astral plane,*" she cautioned. "*My body is asleep in my bed.*"

I'll be fine," he assured her. "*Just give me a moment to create an avatar of myself.*" Stretching out his tiny hands toward the cell, a stream of gold slipped under the wall and became an exact replica of Trilllium lying on a bed. "*I'm ready now,*" he said. "*Take me to my brother.*"

Chapter 9
Introducing Trillium

As Tamara stretched in her bed, she looked at Savea lying next to her and asked, *"Did all that just happen?"*

"Look in your pocket and see if he's in there," suggested Savea. Tamara reached into her pocket and pulled out the tiny body of Trillium. She gently set him down on the floor and waited. There was a purple flash and he stood before them as a full-sized man.

"That's amazing!" cried Tamara. *"You are a truly talented magician. I hope you will be able to help my father achieve his potential."*

"I will do my best," he promised.

Hearing a knock at the door, Tamara hurried to answer it. Pulling the door open, she was surprised to find the Commander standing there. *"I hope I'm not intruding,"* he said, walking into the room. Glancing around the room, he stopped in front of Trillium and looked puzzled. *"I just left you in my office,"* he asserted. *"How did you get here before me?"*

Before Trillium could respond, Tamara touched the Commander's arm and said, *"This is not my father,*

Commander. This is his twin brother, Trillium."

"*So your astral journey was successful, then?*" remarked the Commander. "*But how did you manage to bring him here?*"

"*I don't know,*" admitted Tamara. "*He can make himself very small and then he asked me to put him in my pocket. When Savea and I awoke upon our return, I retrieved him from my pocket and set him on the floor. There was a purple flash—and there he was, full sized!*"

"*I'm amazed—and very impressed,*" expressed the Commander. "*Trillium, welcome to Marinea. I'm sure your brother will be thrilled to meet you. I'll send him a message to come here immediately.*"

"*Do you always communicate mentally here?*" asked Trillium.

The Commander answered, "*We do, as a security precaution. We have had listening devices to contend with.*"

Another knock at the door and Trident walked in. His face showed astonishment, and then a welcoming smile. Moving toward Trillium, he clasped him by the shoulders and said, "*At last we meet! I'm assuming that you are real, and not an avatar!*"

Tamara held her glasses out so her father could put them on. "*Here, Father. See for yourself.*"

Trident donned the glasses and sighed, *"I'm so relieved! We have years of experiences to share! It's almost time for dinner. Shall we proceed to the Private Dining Room?"*

"I'll message the rest of our committee and meet you there, Sire," promised the Commander.

*   *   *   *   *

At dinner, the conversation was lively and informative. Trillium's stories of his childhood were both appalling and inspiring. *"You have overcome so many obstacles,"* approved Trident. *"And your magical abilities are a wonder to behold. I hope that you will be willing to help me increase my magical proficiency. I have had a very late start, since everyone assumed that I was a nonmagical."*

"Take my hand," instructed Trillium. Trident complied and a golden haze surrounded them. When Trillium released his brother's hand, he said, *"You now share every ability that I possess. It will not take long to bring you up to speed on how to use them."*

"Seriously?" asked Trident. *"When dinner is finished, let's go into the Practice Field and begin my education."*

*   *   *   *   *

After Trident and Trillium left for the Practice Field, the remaining members of the "committee" decided to order dessert and continue their conversation.

Tamara presented her major concern, *"We don't know when Sunan will attack. His original plan of substituting Trillium for Father is no longer viable."*

"That appears to be true," agreed Savea. *"But how confident are you in Trillium's loyalty? We really don't know him. At one point, we trusted Sunan, and look how that turned out."*

"Commander," pressed Savea, *"in the past, you created some potions that would color a person's skin if he was lying. Both Brothers passed that test. What do you think happened?"*

"Their powers are significantly more effective than mine," he offered. *"They probably neutralized the potions before drinking them."*

"Trillium is an incredibly powerful magician," said Solange. *"Couldn't he neutralize such an effort as well?"*

"Of course," admitted the Commander. *"But perhaps not if the potion were created by Super Beings such as you and Savea."*

"Or if I were allowed by the Creator Being to strengthen the Sisters' potion," suggested Terra.

"If the Creator Being approved and aided such an act," affirmed Tamara, *"I would be comfortable with the outcome."*

Terra nodded and hurried from the dining room.

*   *   *   *   *

The next day, the "committee" once again gathered at breakfast. Trident and Trillium had excused themselves to return to the Practice Field. Terra hurried in to join them and was the bearer of good news.

"The Creator Being believes that truth is essential at this point and has given me a flask of wine that will compel anyone who drinks even a drop to tell the absolute truth," she assured them.

"Even if it is diluted within a normal glass of wine?" asked Tamara.

"Yes," Terra affirmed.

"That will be a very useful tool," approved the Commander. *"Shall we have a cocktail party tonight prior to dinner?"*

"I think that is a marvelous idea," Tamara agreed. *"I'd like it to be a small and intimate gathering. What do you think about holding it on the balcony overlooking the garden?"*

"That's a perfect spot," said Solange. *"Until then, think of what we need to know and how it can be tactfully expressed."*

Chapter 10
The Cocktail Party

Tamara came to the cocktail party in a festive mood. She had dressed for the occasion in an aquamarine velvet floor-length gown and wore a tiara of pearls on her hair. Noting that both Trident and Trillium had already arrived and were chatting amiably as they enjoyed the view of the garden, she walked to the bar and picked up two glasses of the wine that she had previously prepared. Smiling, she offered the wine to each of the brothers and returned to the bar to get a glass for herself.

Raising her glass in a toast, she offered a few words of welcome to Trillium and asked about their session that morning in the practice field. Trident praised his brother's prowess as a teacher and Trillium returned the compliment by relating how well his student was progressing. *"In other words, you two are quite a formidable team,"* she chuckled. *"I'm impressed."*

Just then, the Commander entered with a Super Sister on each arm. *"We're ready to party!"* exclaimed Savea as she headed toward the bar. Soon the wine and the conversation was flowing and everyone seemed to be having a good time.

Solange strolled over to where Trillium was standing and queried, "*May I ask you a personal question?*"

"*Of course,*" he replied. "*I have nothing to hide.*"

She looked into his eyes and probed, "*You have had a challenging life, quite unlike the one my son has experienced. Do you have any feelings of envy or resentment toward him?*"

"*Of course I do,*" he responded. "*But neither of us has fault in what has transpired. We are fortunate to have the opportunity to meet and share a life now that is beneficial to both of us.*"

Solange felt truth in his words and relaxed.

Ever vigilant, Trina entered the party wearing her glasses and the blue cloak. Walking to the bar, she observed that the doctored wine glowed and she selected a glass that did not. As she raised it to her lips, her cloak morphed into a waistband and she dropped her glass where it shattered on the floor.

Tamara hurried to her side and asked, "*Trina, is something the matter?*"

Trina nodded and silently alerted her sister to the danger in the wine. The Commander joined them immediately and announced that dinner was about to be served. As the twins moved toward the entrance to the private dining room, Trina briefed the Commander on the present danger. The Commander called his aide and ordered that all wine be collected and analyzed immediately. Meanwhile, he cast a spell on the entire group that would neutralize any ill effects of the already consumed wine.

*   *   *   *   *

After dinner, the Commander invited Trillium to come to his office for a short chat. Trillium agreed and the two men walked together to the Commander's office. Once inside, they sat in chairs across from each other near a table where a decanter of wine and two glasses had been placed.

The Commander poured out two glasses and offered one to Trillium. Trillium paused, then accepted the glass and took a sip. *"This wine is excellent, Commander, and fortified,"* he commented.

"Fortified?" asked the Commander.

"Yes, with the same substance that was added to my drink in the cocktail party," Trillium added.

"How did you know that?" asked the Commander. *"Did you neutralize or otherwise alter your drink?"*

"Of course I did," admitted Trillium. *"I didn't know what effect it might have on me."*

"And have you also altered the drink in your hand?" probed the Commander.

"*I'm a skilled magical, Commander,*" insisted Trillium, "*but something new has been added to my drink that I've been unable to identify.*"

"*That is correct,*" agreed the Commander. "*But please be assured that there is nothing harmful in your drink—only a potion that guarantees truth.*

"*Now I have a series of important questions to ask you. Are you ready?*" asked the Commander.

"*Certainly,*" replied Trillium. "*I have nothing to hide.*"

"*Then let us proceed,*" said the Commander. "*First, do you have any hostile intent toward your twin brother or this kingdom?*"

"*I do not.*"

"*What about toward the Queen or the Super Sisters? You told Solange that you do have feelings of envy and resentment toward your brother.*"

"*I did, but I also assured her that neither of us had any fault in the differences in our backgrounds. I also emphasized that I value the opportunity to share our lives going forward.*"

"*I would like to place you in a relaxed meditative state so that I can locate any memories that may have been suppressed without your knowledge. Is that acceptable?*" asked the Commander.

"*I give you permission,*" replied Trillium. "*May I lie*

down on that couch?"

"*Of course,*" agreed the Commander, as he guided Trillium to the couch. Once Trillium was comfortable, the Commander began chanting and extended his arms until a green haze emerged and covered Trillium's head. What looked like a vid screen appeared showing Sunan casting a spell on Trillium. Sunan's words were so soft that the Commander had difficulty hearing them, so he augmented his own spell to increase the sound. His face displayed both concentration and dismay as he realized what Sunan had done.

Releasing Trillium from the meditative state, the Commander shared with him what he had discovered.

"*Trillium, Sunan made you into an undercover spy,*" the Commander began. "*He allowed you to be freed by us so that you could follow his instructions once you were in our kingdom.*"

"What?" cried Trillium. "*What have I done?*"

"*Not only did you reverse the potion placed in the wine at the cocktail party, but you substituted it with another spell that Sunan gave you. That spell was designed to put everyone into a deep sleep in 48 hours so that the invasion could be swift and without challenge. We are approaching that time very soon.*"

"*What can we do?*" exclaimed Trillium.

"I will show you the memory and, hopefully, you will be able to neutralize the spell." The Commander restored the memory on the screen and Trillium watched it carefully.

"Is there some way I can communicate with everyone who attended the cocktail party?" he asked.

"I think we need to call Tamara to join us immediately," replied the Commander. *"She may be able to do so with the help of her crystals."* Sending an urgent message to Tamara, the two men began exchanging ideas on how to proceed.

Several minutes later, Tamara knocked at the Commander's door and entered, along with Terra. *"I thought that Mother, as a Watcher, should be included in our conversation,"* she explained.

"A Watcher?" asked Trillium. *"Your Mother is a Watcher?"*

"Yes, I am," said Terra. *"Is that a problem?"*

"No, I'm just surprised," replied Trillium. *"No wonder Tamara is so powerful! Does that mean that you will report everything we say and do?"*

"If it's relevant," she responded.

"I hope it doesn't get me into trouble," he worried.

"Why, what have you done?" asked Tamara.

The Commander briefed them on what he had discovered about Sunan's spell that had required Trillium to act without knowing or remembering his actions. *"And now,"* he added, *"we have to send a message to everyone at that cocktail party immediately before the spell activates. Tamara, can you do that?"*

"I'll try," she replied, touching her forehead. *"But I also need the spell that will neutralize what has been cast."*

"That's it!" cried the Commander. *"You don't have to do that. I just have to put Trillium in an isolation cell until the time runs out! Remember what happened to Sostor's spell!"*

"Of course!" she replied. *"Trillium, when Sostor was placed in an isolation cell, a spell he had cast ceased functioning."*

"In case that doesn't work," urged the Commander, *"please communicate with the party participants and ask them to keep in touch with us for the next 24 hours."*

"And meanwhile," added Terra, *"I must leave you for a short time. I will return as soon as I can."*

"Where did your mother go?" asked Trillium.

"Probably to report in," answered Tamara.

"Where? To whom?" pressed Trillium.

"To the Creator Being," she replied.

Trillium stared at her. *"She knows the Creator Being?"*

"All Watchers do," said the Commander, as he aimed his memory-eraser device at Trillium and pressed the flash.

Next he took Trillium's arm and escorted him to an isolation cell, promising to retrieve him when the spell had expired.

Chapter 11
Unexpected Discoveries

After a day passed, the Commander felt comfortable releasing Trillium from the isolation cell. There had been no reports of party participants falling into a mysterious sleep. However, it was unknown whether Sunan had a way to confirm whether his spell had worked.

The Commander brought Trillium back to his office for another chat. With Trillium's permission, he resumed his interrogation, including inducing a dream state. This time, his questions were more specific and direct. He needed to be certain that all information had been secured.

Once Trillium had relaxed on the couch, the Commander cast a spell that would assure truthful responses and identify half-truths. It appeared that Trillium had no memory of being the victim of Sunan's magic. However, he was not certain that a 'infiltrating' spell had not been part of Sunan's plan.

In order to rule that out, he began to chant a little-known spell that he had learned years ago. Part of the spell involved rendering the subject unconscious. When he had done so, he spoke to Trillium's spirit and asked whether any orders or restraints had been assigned to it. A spirit responded, but in an entirely different voice. The Commander was shocked when he discovered that a malevolent spirit had been placed within Trillium and was subject to Sunan's will. Shaking his head, he sent a mental plea to Tamara. He would need her help.

*   *   *   *   *

Tamara hurried through his office door. "*Your call sounded urgent. Has something happened?*" she asked.

The Commander related the details of his interaction with the unconscious Trillium and asked for her advice. "*I'm in unfamiliar territory,*" she admitted, "*but it sounds like an exorcism is required. The Sisters could be useful to us. I'll call them.*"

*   *   *   *   *

When the Sisters arrived, Tamara briefed them on Trillium's condition and her belief that Sunan had been experimenting with dark magic. She asked them if they had any experience with exorcisms. Savea blushed and admitted that when she was angry with Solange, she had done some investigation of dark magic. "I never intended to use it, but I was intrigued with its possibilities," she said. "*Tamara, ask your mother to join us. This definitely falls within her skill set.*"

"*Really?*" wondered Tamara. "*I would never have*

68

guessed." When she issued the call, Terra appeared in the office with them.

"*You don't need to tell me what's going on,*" Terra explained. "*I've been monitoring Trillium's activities.*"

"*So you haven't trusted him, then?*" asked Tamara.

"*He's an unknown quantity and it's my duty to observe and report,*" clarified Terra. "*I do agree with you, Tamara, that an exorcism is advised. I need to check in with the Creator Being and come right back.*"

Terra disappeared and, before they could even continue their conversation, she had returned. "*I've been given the authority and skills to conduct an exorcism. Let us proceed.*"

"*Before you do,*" said the Commander, "*I need to contact my aide.*" He placed the call and in a few minutes, his aide knocked at the door. "*Please go to the isolation cell holding Sostor. Stay and observe him and report any changes.*" The aide nodded and left immediately.

Terra walked to Trillium's side and began to slowly chant a spell that no one recognized. She placed one hand on his forehead and the other on his chest. He began to resist her and uttered guttural cries. The Sisters came to Terra's aid and held him down on the couch.

As Terra continued to chant, Trillium began to scream and his mouth opened wide. A black smoke erupted from his mouth and hovered over his body. The Commander picked up a large glass container from his desk and handed it to Terra. She accepted it gratefully and held it beneath the smoke, which began to sink into the container. In a few minutes, all the smoke had relocated into the container, which the Commander covered with a secure lid. He assured everyone that the container and lid were especially constructed to hold evil entities.

Trillium sat up, gasping. *"What has happened?"* he asked, looking at the container with dread. Terra held his hand and gently explained that he had been possessed, without his consent, by Sunan. *"The spirit captured in this jar was evil and subject to Sunan's every whim,"* she explained. *"You would have been forced to obey its orders."*

Shaking visibly, Trillium sank back on the couch. He thanked Terra profusely for saving him and kept apologizing to everyone in the room. *"Are you sure there is nothing evil left in me?"* he asked wearily.

"I'm sure," answered Terra. *"I followed the Creator Being's instructions precisely. However, I am not finished. I am to accompany Tamara on an astral journey to Mesarra and release this spirit in front of Sunan, with the directive that it enter Sunan's body and self-destruct."*

"Will it obey you?" asked Tamara.

"*Oh yes,*" replied Terra. "*It has no choice.*"

*   *   *   *   *

Several minutes later, Tamara and Terra reached Tamara's room with the container and lay down on the bed. Holding hands, they drifted into a dream state and headed toward Mesarra. Soon they spied sand dunes in the distance and flew toward the palace.

Entering the palace through a side door, they located Sunan in the throne room. Armed robot guards were stationed along the walls. At first, Sunan didn't notice that he had visitors, but his attention soon focused on the two women.

"Well, well, well," he sneered. "I warned you that I could detect your presence, Tamara. Why are you here?"

"We are here on a mission, assigned by the Creator Being," she replied.

"We?" he questioned. "I see only you."

Terra walked toward the throne and opened the container. The smoke containing the evil spirit spiraled into Sunan's chest and the self-destruct process began. "What have you done?" he wailed. "Your judgment has been decided," pronounced Terra and she rejoined Tamara. Holding hands with her mother, Tamara touched her crystal and they instantly returned to her bed. Tamara snuggled into her covers and Terra placed a kiss on her forehead. "*Sleep well, my daughter.*"

*   *   *   *   *

The phone on the Commander's desk rang. When he answered it, he learned from his aide that Sostor had suddenly disappeared and the Sostor avatar had also vanished. As he thanked his aide for the update, he relaxed back in his chair and smiled, "So it is true. If one half dies, the other also perishes. So be it."

Chapter 12
Justice Has Been Served

The next morning, the "committee" gathered in the Private Dining Room for breakfast, as had been the custom now for some time. Tamara and Terra briefed the group about their astral journey to Mesarra. The Commander related his news about Sostor's demise. Trillium added insights into his experience with the exorcism.

Tamara summarized: *"It was an eventful day, and a stressful one. Mother, Sunan said again that he could see me. Why couldn't he see you?"*

"Because I'm a Watcher, dear. We can only be seen if we allow it," Terra explained.

Trident had been sitting next to his brother and put his arm around Trillium's shoulders. *"How are you, Brother?"*

"I'm still processing the events of yesterday," Trillium admitted. *"And I certainly wasn't aware that when one Super Twin dies, the other would also do so. Did all of you know that would happen?"*

Solange and Savea nodded. *"Remember that we were originally one being, so that was not a surprise to us."*

Trina interjected, "*I didn't realize that would happen. I guess I never thought about it. But I do have a question: Who will rule those two land kingdoms now that the Super Brothers are gone?*"

Terra reminded them that Rogere, who had been the male Watcher/Parent to the current Super Children, had been transferred to Mosshire when Sostor was captured. "*Another male Watcher will be assigned to the Crystal Castle in his place,*" she added. "*Rogere has been ruler of Mosshire on a temporary basis, but I understand he will assume that role permanently. He is well-regarded by the residents.*"

"*But what about Mesarra?*" continued Trina. "*What will happen there?*"

"*That is still under discussion,*" responded Terra. "*However, one name has been seriously considered.*"

"*Don't keep us in suspense, Mother!*" laughed Tamara. "*Who is it?*"

"*Before I tell you, what qualifications do you think would be important for such a nominee?*" she replied.

Trident answered, "*As someone who has led a kingdom, I would hope that the nominee would be kind and fair, knowledgeable about the needs and welfare of the population, and a genuinely good person. Of course, leadership is also important, but I have to note that I had no experience when I became King. Plus, even though I ruled as a non-magical, I would hope that the successful candidate would possess a high level of magical skills."*

"A good answer," approved Terra. *"Do we know anyone who meets those qualifications?"*

Solange and Savea exclaimed in unison: *"Trilllium!"*

"What?" exclaimed Trillium. *"Are you serious?"*

"We are!" agreed the Sisters.

Solange added, *"You share those qualities with your brother, plus your magical prowess is legendary."*

Savea commented, *"And you have spent much of your life in Mesarra, so your knowledge of the country and its needs is second to none."*

"Trillium, it is good to hear such support from your family," smiled Terra, *"especially since I have just been informed that you have been appointed the new ruler of Mesarra!"*

Jumping from their chairs, the entire group swarmed Trillium with congratulations. He looked stunned as he accepted their good wishes. When everyone was seated again, he looked at Trident and begged, *"Brother, would you consider traveling to Mesarra with me and serving as my adviser until I grow into the role?"*

"I'd be honored," Trident agreed, clasping Trillium's

hand.

"*That's an excellent idea,*" Terra murmured, "*especially since I'm being relocated to Mesarra to help you settle in. I hope that's agreeable to you.*"

"*I feel much more comfortable now,*" Trillium admitted. "*Thank you for welcoming me so warmly.*"

Trina fidgeted in her chair and finally blurted out, "*Mother, Father, I hope you will understand. I want to remain here with Tamara and continue my training with Jon. I can visit you in Mesarra, but I prefer to live here.*"

Terra and Trident exchanged glances and Terra spoke first, "*Of course we understand, dear. You are a grown woman now with increasing talents and magical skills. I would have been surprised if you hadn't made this decision.*"

Trident rose and hugged his daughter as he promised to be available whenever she needed him. He turned to Trillium and asked, "*When would you like to journey to Mesarra, Brother? I will need to wind up some projects here.*"

Trillium asked Terra if any schedule had been suggested. She replied that he had some latitude, but that the coronation date had been set for three months from now. "*However, you need to know that there is some cleanup to be done in terms of robots and armaments that Sunan had created,*" she revealed. "*I believe that your magical talent will be very useful."*

"*I could be ready to travel in two weeks,*" said Trident. "*Would that work for you, Brother?*"

"*I still have some contacts there,*" Trillium replied. "*I will arrange for some temporary housing. That will give us time to do some undercover scoping of the area before we have to appear in an official capacity.*"

"*Terra, when do your duties begin in Mesarra?*" asked Trident.

"*Immediately,*" she responded. "*At that point, our paths must not cross until I notify you otherwise.*"

"*You three are making me nervous,*" admitted Tamara. "*Will you be in danger?*"

"*I don't know,*" her mother answered. "*With Sunan gone, the power structure may be unstable. That is why we must move covertly and quietly until we know more about the kingdom and what has occurred since Sunan disappeared. Remember that the former Watchers have been recalled and new ones have not yet been appointed. We are going in blind.*"

Solange looked puzzled. "*If you are being this careful about entering Mesarra, why are you not also being cautious about Mosshire? A new ruler is being installed there as well.*"

Terra explained that the situations are different. "*The new ruler of Mosshire is a very experienced Watcher, not a newly appointed person with no ruling or political background. In addition, Sostor's kingdom was highly regimented and the population was used to an orderly existence. Sunan, on the other hand, let his people do as they wished, while he used technology in secret to fulfill his desires. Therefore, there are major unknowns in Mesarra."*

"That's a long way of saying that we have had eyes on Mosshire, but not on Mesarra," summarized Savea.

"That's not entirely true," commented the Commander. *"I've been watching Mesarra for some time. There is considerable intel available. Trident has already been studying what has been collected."*

Her face etched with worry, Tamara hugged her parents and Trillium, wishing them safe travels and a successful mission. As they left to prepare for their journey, she finally allowed tears to gently slide down her cheeks.

Chapter 13
Mission: Mesarra

Solange and Savea remained with Tamara in the Private Dining Room after the others had left. They sat on either side of her, holding her hands. *"I know this is a difficult thing to ask, my dear,"* expressed Savea, *"but try not to worry. Your parents are highly proficient administrators and Trillium's magic skills are beyond magnificent. As a team, they are formidable."*

Solange added, *"Plus, I suspect that Terra's restrictions on interfering have been waived for this mission. I expect that she will be a very welcome backup for the twins."*

"You do make me feel better," admitted Tamara. *"However, I don't promise to stay here and never check on them astrally—unless my bracelets refuse to take me, of course."*

"That's a future consideration," said Solange. *"For the present, let's do everything we can to help with their preparation and send them off with a spirit of confidence and expectation of success."*

Tamara nodded and walked with the Sisters to begin their day.

*　　*　　*　　*　　*

It was departure day, and Tamara was waiting at the Bubble Train station at the Palace to see her parents and uncle off on their journey. She saw them approaching, escorted by the Sisters and the Commander. Trina was running behind them, and caught up just as they were about to board the train. There were hugs all around as the travelers entered the car reserved for royals. Waving furiously as the train pulled away from the platform, Tamara and Trina hugged each other and watched it disappear from sight.

Tamara sighed and commented that it felt like she was entering a new phase of life. *"I never realized how much I relied on my parents as a source of support. This will be quite an adjustment for me."*

Trina seized Tamara's hands and said, *"Look at me! I'm here for you and my blue cloak is still a cloak—no danger is present. You can relax."*

Tamara nodded gratefully and suggested that they join her for lunch in the Private Dining Room.

*　　*　　*　　*　　*

After a lengthy trip via train and airship, Trident, Terra and Trillium arrived in Mesarra to begin their mission. They were met by Trillium's contact, who had a car ready to take them to their temporary quarters. After settling in, they convened in the foyer and agreed to take a walk to acquaint themselves with their immediate surroundings. The palace was only a short walk away.

After just a brief stroll, they realized that a shopping trip was in order. If they were to remain incognito, they needed to buy clothing that would fit in with the local culture. They soon found a store offering exactly the type of clothing that they were seeking. After purchasing the necessary items, they returned to their quarters and changed into more appropriate attire.

On their shopping trip, they had noticed what seemed to be a small cafe and they headed for it to enjoy a meal and watch locals passing by.

As they sat relaxing, Trident asked whether mental communication would work here without Tamara as a conduit. He also noticed that Terra was staring at him. "*I'm going to try and then I have a suggestion,*" she began, "*The two of you are going to attract attention because you are twins. One of you has to change your appearance.*"

Trillium commented that the telepathy was obviously working, since he understood everything she said. "*Let's toss a coin, Brother, to see which of us will undergo a makeover,*" he added.

Terra tossed a coin in the air and Trident won the toss.

"*I guess I will volunteer you,*" he said. "*Will the locals know if we use magic?*"

Trillium replied, "*They never noticed when I did, so I'll definitely be the makeover subject. Let's see, I'll make my hair dark and curly, and encourage a short beard to grow. Then I'll wear a wide-brimmed hat to keep the sun off. That should do it.*" A few minutes later, his appearance was completely altered.

"*Much better,*" approved Terra. "*And now I must leave you. I will not be staying in your quarters. Accommodations have been arranged for me and I must begin my Watcher duties. I will be in touch occasionally—shall we say in the evening at this cafe on odd numbered days? And if you need me, just call.*"

Trident kissed his wife goodbye and she left the table. When he looked after her, he saw her disappear.

"*Well, Brother,*" he said, "*Shall we resume our surveillance walk?*"

*   *   *   *   *

As they methodically covered the area, there was little to notice as unusual. People seemed to go about their lives without incident: walking, eating, shopping, and so forth. There were no observable examples of magic being used. Trident reached into his pocket for a handkerchief and was surprised to find a pair of glasses instead. *"That Trina,"* he thought. *"She's looking out for me."* He donned the glasses and stopped abruptly.

Looking around, he could see no people at all. He turned to Trillium—and he wasn't there, either! Taking the glasses off, everything seemed back to normal. He sent a mental message to Terra, asking her to meet him immediately. She appeared at once.

"Is there a problem?" she asked with concern.

"Yes," he responded. *"Trina apparently hid these glasses in my pocket and when I put them on, everything around me vanished—even Trillium!"*

She took the glasses from him and looked through them. *"You are correct,"* she affirmed. *"Everything does disappear. That means that nothing is real. But what really worries me is that Trillium is not real. Back in Marinea, when that dark spirit was removed from him, we thought he was back to normal— but that doesn't seem to have been the case. Something else is going on. I have to report in. I'll be right back,"* she said as she vanished. A few minutes later, she returned.

"I'm going to message Tamara and ask her to make an astral journey here. We need her help," she explained.

*   *   *   *   *

Tamara received the summons from her mother as she

was about to retire for the night. Hearing the urgency in the message, she lay down on her bed and began to relax into a dream state. Asking her bracelets to transport her to her mother's side in Mesarra, she felt herself rising above the bed and flying into the sky. It seemed like a very short time before she saw sand dunes in front of her. A few minutes later, she was landing in a street near the palace very close to where her parents were standing.

"*What is wrong?*" she asked her mother.

Terra briefed her on what her father had said and what the Creator Being had told her.

"*I can't believe what I'm hearing!*" exclaimed Tamara. "*Nothing that I think I'm seeing is real? When you threw that evil spirit at Sunan, it didn't self-destruct and kill him? It actually not only preserved him but also drew Sostor from our isolation cell and deposited him here? The Super Brothers are still alive? And the whole conspiracy was engineered by Trillium, who had been lured into dark magic by Sunan?*"

"*You have summarized that brilliantly, daughter,*" admired Trident. "*But the overriding question is: What do we do now?*"

Chapter 14
Black or White?

"We seem to be in a constant state of catch-up," complained Tamara. *"First, we trusted Sunan with valuable intel and now we find out that Trillium has also fooled us completely. Why can we not see through their duplicity?"*

"Never be ashamed of trusting, Tamara," advised Terra. *"The fault is on the liars, not on you."*

"However, the lesson to be learned is to be more cautious in bestowing trust," suggested Trident. *"Terra, did the Creator Being have any recommendation of a path forward here?"*

"Actually, I learned that Tamara was the key to a brighter future, which is why I sent for her. We are charged with discovering how that is to take place," revealed Terra. *"But I am freed from any constraints and may help as needed."*

"If part of the solution includes terminating my twin, I don't know if I can do that," admitted Trident.

"Don't go there, Father," said Tamara. *"We don't know how the future will unfold."*

"I agree," Terra added. *"Let's go to where I am staying*

85

and begin to plan. There is room there for all three of us."

*   ＊   ＊   ＊   ＊   ＊*

As they arrived at Terra's temporary dwelling, Tamara brought up an urgent issue, *"I am only here on the astral plane. I need to return home to recharge periodically. Is there any way to let me remain here for longer periods of time?"* As she asked the question, purple stripes appeared on her bracelets. *"I have a feeling that my bracelets have just responded to my concern."*

"What do you think those stripes mean?" asked Terra.

"I have no idea," replied Tamara. *"If the past is any clue, I will find out when it is necessary."*

"Until then," proposed Terra, *"Would anyone like something to eat or drink? Oh, sorry Tamara, you can't do that, can you?"*

"Frankly, at this point, I really don't know what is or is not possible," she replied.

"Then let's experiment," her mother advised. *"I'll make some tea and sandwiches."*

In a few minutes, they were sitting around a table in the kitchen of Terra's dwelling. A plate of sandwiches and a pot of tea were set in the middle of the table and Tamara and her parents each had a place setting before them.

"Try picking up a sandwich, Tamara," instructed her

86

father. She reached for one and, unlike past experiences, her hand did not pass through it. The sandwich felt solid and normal to her and she attempted to take a bite. She was surprised, but pleased, that she was able to do so. With each additional bite, her image seem to solidify. Even small sips of tea remained with her. She felt her energy increasing as she ingested nourishment and was amazed that this was happening.

Her parents smiled at her astonishment. *"Your bracelets never let you down,"* commented her father. *"I don't think you need to worry about overstaying your ability to react and perform."*

"I'm impressed with the clever way your bracelets are meeting your needs," added her mother. *"They have created a way for you to monitor your capabilities. When you see yourself beginning to fade, that's a signal that you need to reenergize."*

"But not return to my bed?"

"No, I don't believe so," affirmed her mother. *"Your path forward appears to be here with us."*

"So let's review what we have witnessed," suggested Trident. *"I totally believed that the Trillium I met was real, especially after that dark spirit was removed from him. If that was dark magic, it was both powerful and ingenious."*

"I agree," said Terra. *"We were all fooled by him. What*

is unclear is whether he is redeemable or not."

"I think that question needs to be tabled for now," Tamara warned. *"Our more immediate challenge lies with the Super Brothers. They originally seemed to have been influenced by a now erased set of Super Being Parents. However, what they have done recently suggests independent thought and intent. If that is true, and they are no longer being manipulated, do we have the knowledge or ability to vanquish them?"*

"No," Terra admitted. *"But the Creator Being does. Remember that the Super Being parents were erased multiple times—before, hopefully, an appropriate pair was created. I believe that solution can be applied here, as well. I will keep in close contact with the Creator Being as we move forward."*

"The Super Sisters are still with us," reflected Tamara. *"If the Super Brothers are erased, would another set be created in order to maintain balance?"*

"That's an interesting question," acknowledged Terra. *"I'll look into it."*

Trident looked confused. *"We had originally been operating within an assumption that Sostor was my father— mostly because he claimed to be because of what he perceived as a striking resemblance between us. Was any of that true? Or was it part of the game that the Super Parents were playing?*

And, what about our current intel that a mysterious guard named Rogere is my father?"

"*Questions like that make my head hurt, Father,*" sighed Tamara. "*I don't know what is true or false anymore. When the Super Brothers were visiting us and I corrected their imbalance, my bracelets did not detect any falsehoods. If we go down that path, could something have happened to affect them and prompt negative behavior after they returned home?*"

Terra looked stricken. "*The Watchers in both their kingdoms were recalled because of unseemly behavior. How old would Trillium have been at that time?*"

"*The same age as father,*" clarified Tamara. "*I was Queen when the Brothers' behavior changed, so he was an adult—and, reportedly, a master sorcerer!*"

"*I need to report in,*" cried Terra. "*I'll be back soon.*"

*   *   *   *   *

It took longer than they expected for Terra to return. When she reappeared in her kitchen, her eyes were worried. She sat at the table and put her face in her hands. "*Nothing is as it seemed,*" she began. "*I had drawn certain conclusions after observing for a long time. Those conclusions may be false.*"

"*What conclusions?*" asked Trident.

"*As to the identity of your father, for example,*" she

whispered. "*And what—or who—was motivating the Brothers. The Creator Being is displeased with me and has charged me with reexamining the entire situation. I'm so sorry. I'm afraid I let my love for you color my interpretation of what I was seeing.*"

"*What exactly does that mean, Mother?*" asked Tamara.

"*I'm being reassigned to a special task force that has the mission of reassessing the Watcher reports of the last decade,*" she said sorrowfully. "*I can no longer participate in your lives until that mission is accomplished.*" Terra faded before their eyes.

About the Author

After doing academic writing during my 20 years as Professor at the University of Wisconsin-Madison, I retired to Hawai'i in 1999. A decade later, I began being aware of an interesting fantasy story line in my mind and began writing it soon after. It was an occasional hobby for another decade and then the book became impatient with me and began to seriously nudge me. Since I began "listening" to the book, the writing has been a fun and all-encompassing part of my life.

Crystal Saga Series by
D. E. Weingand

Book 1
Tamara's Crystals

Book 2
Genesis Explored

Book 3
Masquerade

Book 4
Discoveries

Book 5
Gamesmanship

Book 6
Beginnings

Book 7
Looking Forward . . . and Backward

Book 8
Making Progress

Scan the QR Code with Your Cell Phone to Order Books

Coming Soon

Book 9
Searching for Truth

Book 10
The Truth is Out There

Book 11
Finding Truth

Book 12
Loose Ends